BROKEN WHEEL RANCH

Clark Hudson saw the mark of outlaw stamped on Fred Hayes' face, yet he could not be perfectly certain that Hayes had committed the murder for which he was being tried in court. Nevertheless, the jury of which Clark was the foreman decided the man was guilty and sent him to jail.

That won for Hudson Hayes' undying enmity, and the gratitude of Jed Porter, owner of the Walking L in Porter Valley. It also brought him an offer to work on Hayes' former spread, the Broken Wheel, which Tom Morton had bought and which he wanted to keep from being swallowed up by Porter.

In such a situation, Clark found it hard to tell friends from enemies. The only thing he could be certain of was that there would be blood on the grass, and that wherever he was working he would be stained by it.

Wayne C. Lee was born to pioneering homesteaders near Lamar, Nebraska. His parents were old when he was born and it was an unwritten law since the days of the frontier that it was expected that the youngest child would care for the parents in old age. Having grown up reading novels by Zane Grey and William MacLeod Raine, Lee wanted to write Western stories himself. His best teachers were his parents. They might not be able to remember what happened last week by the time Lee had reached his majority, but they shared with him their very clear memories of the pioneer days. In fact they talked so much about that period that it sometimes seemed to Lee he had lived through it himself. Lee wrote a short story and let his mother read it. She encouraged him to submit it to a magazine and said she would pay the postage. It was accepted and appeared as *Death Waits at Paradise Pass* in *Lariat Story Magazine.* In the many Western novels that he has written since, violence has never been his primary focus, no matter what title a publisher might give one of his stories, but rather the interrelationships between the characters and within their communities. These are the dominant characteristics in all of Lee's Western fiction and create the ambiance so memorable in such diverse narratives as *The Gun Tamer* (1963), *Petticoat Wagon Train* (1972), and *Arikaree War Cry* (1992). In the truest sense Wayne C. Lee's Western fiction is an outgrowth of his impulse to create imaginary social fabrics on the frontier and his stories are intended primarily to entertain a reader at the same time as to articulate what it was about these pioneering men and women that makes them so unique and intriguing to later generations. His pacing, graceful style, natural sense of humor, and the genuine liking he feels toward the majority of his characters, combined with a commitment to the reality and power of romance between men and women as a decisive factor in making it possible for them to have a better life together than they could ever hope to have apart, are what most distinguish his contributions to the Western story. His latest novel is *Edge of Nowhere* (1996).

BROKEN WHEEL RANCH

Wayne C. Lee

GUNSMOKE

First published in the UK by W. H. Allen

This hardback edition 2008
by BBC Audiobooks Ltd
by arrangement with
Golden West Literary Agency

ISBN 978 1 405 68139 1

British Library Cataloguing in Publication Data available.

Printed and bound in Great Britain by
Antony Rowe Ltd., Chippenham, Wiltshire

CHAPTER I

Clark Hudson had lived through some rugged days, but none that had tried his mental endurance more than this one. The judge had handed the case to the jury at ten o'clock this morning and now, at the end of seven hours of debating and balloting, they had finally reached a decision.

Clark, leading the other eleven men out to the jury box, looked at the prisoner and the hundred or more faces that jammed the courtroom. The decision hadn't been easy and Clark experienced a fleeting moment of doubt that it was unquestionably right. Neither side had been able to present air-tight testimony.

As the men filed silently to their seats and the judge rapped his gavel for order, Clark studied the prisoner. Fred Hayes was about thirty, a little on the dumpy side, and Clark, who had sized up a lot of men in his twenty-eight years, saw the mark of the outlaw stamped on the man's face. But the evidence presented the last two days in this case left room for a faint doubt, a doubt that it had taken the jury seven hours of debate to dispel.

The judge, his face stern, rapped his gavel again and stared at the jury. "Has the jury reached a decision?" he asked in the sudden silence.

Clark, as foreman of the jury, stepped forward. He was a tall man, two inches over six feet, with broad shoulders that carried his two hundred pounds so well that he had the appearance of being slim. His steady grey eyes ignored the courtroom now and centred on the judge.

"Yes, Your Honour. We find the defendant guilty."

A muffled roar swept over the room and the judge hammered his gavel threateningly. Clark saw the satisfaction on the faces of old Jed Porter and the men around him. Porter, owner of the Walking L in Porter Valley, up in the north-west corner of the county, fifty miles from the county seat, was a neighbour of Fred Hayes' Broken Wheel.

The judge finally restored order and called for the defendant to face the bench. Then in heavy tones he pronounced the fate of the prisoner.

"This court, having found you guilty of second-degree murder, sentences you to twenty years in the state penitentiary in Lincoln."

The judge adjourned court before the roar of the crowd got out of hand again. The sheriff pulled Hayes toward the side door leading to the jail. Hayes jerked back, gritting his teeth as he stared over the crowd.

"I'll get even with you!" he screamed, his face flushed. "I'll get out and I'll make you pay for this!"

Clark wondered whom he had in mind. He wasn't looking at the jury when he said it, and none of the witnesses who had testified against him was in sight just then. Clark was still thinking of that last outburst of Hayes' when the sheriff pulled the prisoner out of the courtroom.

Clark left the jury box and worked his way toward the door. He wanted to get out of the stuffy little courthouse and breathe some fresh air again. He wasn't put together right to thrive cooped up in a building.

He picked up his gun from the deputy sheriff, buckled it on, and stepped out into the street. He stopped there, watching the men file out and head for their rigs and saddle horses up and down the street. He was debating whether to try to ride out to the Circle C tonight or get a room in the hotel when a hand dropped on his shoulder.

"You're Clark Hudson, aren't you?"

Clark wheeled to look at a big man, heavier than Clark but not so tall. His face was seamed by the weather and there was a cool calculating glint in his greenish-blue eyes.

Clark nodded. "That's right. But you've got the best of me."

The other man grinned. "You've probably never seen me before. I'm Tom Morton. I own the Flying M twenty miles east of here."

Clark had heard of the Flying M and its owner. "I stopped at your place looking for a job before I hired on with Calhoun," Clark said. "You were gone that day."

"Too bad," Morton said. "If you were working for me now, it would make things simpler. Are you staying in town tonight?"

"I might. Haven't made up my mind yet."

"Stay," Morton said with a tone of authority. "I'll be over to see you at the hotel right after supper. I've got a proposition you won't want to pass up."

Morton turned and disappeared into the crowd in the direction of the drug store. Clark headed toward the post office, wondering about Morton and the proposition he spoke of.

At the post office, which was in a corner of the grocery store, he asked for his mail and got one letter. Outside, he stopped on the porch and tore open the envelope. He was almost afraid to read the letter, yet he had to know what it said. He had already recognized his sister's handwriting.

"We took Carl to the specialist yesterday," Clark read "He says he'll have to have an operation or he'll lose the use of his arm or maybe worse. But the operation will cost at least six hundred dollars."

Clark held the letter in his hand but his eyes wandered up the main street without seeing the row of buildings on either side. It was up to him to get the money for his brother's operation.

As he stood staring unseeingly at the town, the last few years flashed before him. He recalled the ranch in Kansas where he and his brother and sister had settled with their father. They had done well there until a big rancher started gobbling up everything in sight. The Hudson place had been in sight and it was gobbled up. Not without a fight, the fighting had been futile. And in the battle Jim Hudson, Clark's father, had been killed.

A bitterness had been born in Clark that day that had left its mark on him. When another rancher moved in on that range and a fight loomed, Clark hired his guns to the new man. His younger brother, Carl, had gone along but he lacked the enthusiasm for the job that Clark had. The battle had been a vicious one and Clark Hudson had been instrumental in carrying the new rancher to victory. But Carl had caught a bullet in the arm that threatened now to leave him a permanent cripple.

That had been a year ago. The doctors had said then that an operation must be performed some day. Clark felt it was up to him to get the money for the operation. Hiring his gun wasn't the answer. The risk of meeting a bullet head on was too great and the jobs, while paying well, were too infrequent. A steady job was the answer, and Clark had come to this new country in western Nebraska looking for that job. He had it on the Circle C, but it was going to take a long time to save enough money for that operation on Carl's arm. And, from the tone of Amy's letter, that operation couldn't be postponed much longer if it was to be successful.

He stirred and left the porch, moving down the street to the hotel. Victor was an ordinary cowtown. Clark had seen dozens of them. Just the essentials were here: drug store, hardware, grocery, barber shop, blacksmith, hotel and post office. Some other businesses were moving in now with the coming of the homesteaders.

He went into the hotel, realizing suddenly that there was no longer any question in his mind about staying in town for the night. He got a room, then went into the dining-room for supper. Later, he went up to his room to wait for Tom Morton.

Morton wasn't long in showing up. When Clark opened the door, he came in quickly and found a chair. Pulling out a fat cigar, he lit it and settled back as though he intended to stay a while.

"Don't usually smoke them," he said, fingering the cigar. "But I'm not a drinking man, so I splurge on cigars when I get to town. Besides, I've just closed a deal that calls for a celebration."

Clark said nothing. Morton's dealings were none of his business. He wondered what purpose Morton had in telling about his personal business. Clark had him figured as a man who made few statements he might later regret.

"I know you're wondering what kind of a proposition I've got to offer you," Morton said through a cloud of smoke. "I'm not a man to mince words. I've got a man-sized job I want done, and you're the man to do it."

"I've got a job on the Circle C," Clark reminded him.

Morton nodded. "I know. But you're not tied there. I bought the Broken Wheel from Fred Hayes. I want you to run it for me."

Surprise rocked Clark. "I thought Jed Porter would get that place if Hayes sold."

"Everybody thought that, including Porter. But Hayes would have died rather than see Jed Porter get it."

"Hayes had to sell, so you stepped in?"

Morton nodded. "Exactly. He figured he was going up for a stretch. He wanted somebody on the Broken Wheel who would keep Porter off."

Clark frowned. "Why don't you run it?"

"I've got my place east of here. But the Broken Wheel
B.W.R.—1*

offers a wonderful opportunity and I couldn't pass up the chance to get it. But it's going to be a tough job holding it. That's why I want you to run it."

Clark got up from his seat on the edge of the bed and went to the window to stare out into the night. "Why me?"

"I know what you can do," Morton said easily. "A friend of mine was in that scrap in Kansas. He told me about you. If any man can hold his own against Porter, you're the one."

"I don't want any part of another range war," Clark said, turning to face Morton. "The last one crippled my brother. He's got to have an operation now or be a cripple for life. The next fight might have my number on it."

Morton leaned forward in his chair. "I don't want a scrap, Hudson. And the only way I can prevent it is to send a man up there they'll be afraid to tangle with. If I sent up some weak-kneed saddle bum, they'd run him out before the sun went down. I aim to make the Broken Wheel into a paying proposition. I can't do it with a range war on my hands."

"One man, regardless of his reputation, isn't going to stop a big outfit like Jed Porter's Walking L," Clark said.

Morton puffed on his cigar a moment: "I think he will. Porter's no fool. And he knows he'd be a dead fool if he tangled with the wrong man. If anybody can prevent a war, you're the one. And if no one can stop it, you're the one I'd like to have there when the bullets start flying. How about it? You'll make more than forty a month."

At the mention of pay, a surge of interest rose in Clark. He needed money and he needed it now. He crossed to the bed again and sat down. "How much?"

"One-half the profits of the Broken Wheel."

"There's no profit in a war."

"I know. That will give you added incentive to see that

there is no war. That little spread is the best layout in the entire western end of the state. The profits could be enormous."

"So could the fight to control it. The better anything is, the harder men will fight to own it. Anyway, how do I know you'll stay by your word?"

Morton smiled. "I didn't intend for you to take my word. We'll put it in a contract. And before you decide definitely, you can inquire around about me. You'll find my word is good."

Clark slowly shook his head. "I wouldn't get any money from the profits for at least a year. I've got to have some right away for Carl's operation."

Morton shrugged. "That can be arranged. If you decide to take the job, I'll give you what you need for your brother's operation. It will be a loan on your share of the profits. Fair enough?"

Clark didn't answer for a minute. Getting the money for Carl's operation had been Clark's biggest problem. Now it could be solved in one sweep.

"What if there is no profit?" Clark asked finally.

"There will be," Morton said confidently.

Clark was remembering Jed Porter and the hardness of the man. "Not if there's a scrap."

"If war can't be avoided and our first year's profits are wiped out, we'll cancel the loan and consider it your wages for the year."

Clark took another turn around the room. "Just what will be my job?" he asked.

"Manager of the ranch. I'll be up as often as I can make it, but you'll be the real boss. You were raised on a ranch; you know the business. Calhoun tells me you're a very dependable hand on his Circle C. I'll trust your judgment in running things. I'll bring up the cattle and a crew to work for you."

"What will Calhoun say about me quitting?

"What can he say? He doesn't have you tied down. He knows I'm making you this offer. I told him."

"Looks like you've hired a man," Clark said.

Morton stood up and held out his hand. "Good. You're all I needed to make this day a real success. Ever been up in Porter Valley?"

"No." After sealing the bargain with a handshake, Clark sat back down on the bed. "I'd like to know a little something about it before I go barging in."

"I've been there only once," Morton said reflectively. "But I know the story well. Jed Porter has lived there for several years. Fred Hayes moved in on Spring Creek and homesteaded. In fact, he homesteaded the spring itself where the creek starts running. Porter had always used the creek for watering his stock. Hayes let him keep on using it. There were half a dozen other settlers with Hayes. They settled down the creek from him and took in every foot of that stream all the way to Antelope Creek.

"After they'd been on their land a year, they paid out on their homesteads and got a clear title. Then Hayes bought out the other nesters and set up the Broken Wheel. But you heard most of that at the trial."

Clark nodded. "Some of it. But they tried to twist everything they said at the trial to prove their points. I'm still a little confused about how it all happened."

"Well," Morton went on, "when Hayes got control of all the creek, he started fencing it in and shutting Porter's cattle off from water. That's when the old man hit the sky. Why he didn't foresee that long before is more than I can understand, but apparently he was sure Hayes wouldn't cut him off from the creek. He made threats, and you know the rest. It ended with Hayes killing old Jed's nephew along that fence."

"Then the Broken Wheel has about a thousand acres and ten or twelve miles of boundary."

Morton nodded. "That's right. But it's got the best land in the entire valley. Plenty of good grass and water to run a hundred or more head of stock. And it may grow."

Clark studied the big rancher. "Are you figuring on crowding Porter?"

Morton held up a hand. "Nothing like that. I told you I wanted peace. But if Porter finds he can't have the whole valley, he may pull stakes. If he does, I'll be ready with a standing offer to buy him out."

"I don't want any part in trying to squeeze somebody out."

"There'll be nothing like that. I'll drive a tight bargain if I get the chance, but I won't do any underhanded business. But with Spring Creek for a starter, I wouldn't be surprised if some day I owned that entire valley."

Looking at the rancher, Clark decided he wouldn't be surprised, either. But he wondered what Morton's tactics would be. As boss, he'd keep a tight rein on things or call for his time.

Morton got out of his chair again. "Well, Hudson, I'll see you at the bank when it opens in the morning, and we can make out our agreement papers and I'll give you the money you need for you brother's operation. I'd like to have you get up to the Broken Wheel as soon as you can. There are some good buildings at the spring. I'd hate to have them destroyed."

"You're looking for trouble then?"

Morton turned at the door. "I always look for it. That's the best way to avoid it."

Tom Morton went out and down the stairs, and Clark dropped back on the bed to think over this new hand Fate had dealt him. He was still sitting there when a knock on the door roused him. Habit sent his hand to his gun belt on the back of the chair. But he withdrew it instantly.

"Who's there?" he asked.

"A lady to see you, Mr. Hudson," a feminine voice replied.

For a moment, Clark sat motionless. Why would a lady be coming to his hotel room to see him? He didn't even know any ladies in Victor except the waitress down in the dining room. He crossed to the door and opened it.

A girl Clark guessed to be about twenty-five stood there, her brown eyes twinkling as she saw the surprise on his face. He recognized her instantly. She had been on the witness stand for a short time during Fred Hayes' trial as a defence witness. But in Clark's opinion she helped the state's case more than she had Hayes.

"What are you doing here, Miss Hayes?" he asked bluntly.

Milly Hayes smiled. "Is that the way to greet a lady? Aren't you going to invite me in?"

"In?" Clark repeated.

"I know it's not conventional," she said quickly. "But then I'm not conventional." Her face sobered. "I've got business to talk over with you."

Clark stepped back to let her in. It seemed everyone suddenly had business with him. If he remembered correctly, this girl had said at the trial that she was a cousin of Fred Hayes. In that case, her business with him, foreman of the jury that had convicted Hayes, wouldn't be pleasant.

"Have a chair," he said, motioning to the chair Morton had left not long ago.

She sat down and watched him cross to his seat on the bed. "I saw Tom Morton come out of the hotel. Was he up here?"

"Could be," Clark said slowly. "Why?"

"He bought Fred's place. He has no business with it."

"Money talks when it comes to buying things. And apparently Tom Morton had the money."

"He can't handle the Broken Wheel. He's got a ranch east of here."

Clark nodded. "So I heard. He might hire somebody to run one of the places."

Milly Hayes looked calculatingly at Clark. "I think he did. Or he tried to. Did you take the job?"

Caution tugged at Clark. "What makes you think he asked me?"

"I wasn't born yesterday. If I was in Morton's place, I'd look for a man to run the Broken Wheel who was strong enough to do it. You're that man."

"I suppose I should feel complimented."

Milly took off her hat, letting the lamplight play on her raven hair. "Not necessarily. It's a cold fact. Facts are all I consider. I know Morton was here. He asked you to run the Broken Wheel. Did you take the job?"

There was no dodging the issue, Clark saw. Milly Hayes had a way of seeing right through a man.

He nodded. "I took it. The wages are good."

"Not good enough. You'll be sorry you took that job." Her eyes were like smouldering fires. "There's going to be blood on the grass up in Porter Valley. It could be your blood."

He ran a finger along his chin. "So Morton hinted. But it won't be any skin off your nose."

"I'm not sure of that. Morton ought to stay where he belongs."

Clark looked closely at the girl. "Did you want the Broken Wheel?"

"Why not?" she said frankly. "After all, if Fred was going to get rid of it, why shouldn't he let his cousin have a chance to buy it?"

Clark shrugged. "Sounds reasonable. But the fact is, Tom Morton bought it. There isn't much you can do about that."

Milly leaned forward in her chair and her eyes seemed to burn into Clark. "There is always something that can be done if a person has any gumption. If you didn't take the job of running the Broken Wheel for Morton, he'd be up against it."

"Are you trying to get me to quit a job before I start it?"

Milly nodded. "Exactly."

"Morton would get somebody else," Clark said.

"He wouldn't and you know it," Milly said positively. "That isn't a job that just any man can do."

Clark considered the girl a minute before he answered. "If I quit Morton, what would you gain?"

"I know Tom Morton. He's after the dollar any way he can get it. He knows that if you don't manage the Broken Wheel for him, he'll never be able to get any profit from it. He'd sell out and quick."

"If Morton couldn't find a man who could run the place, how would you do it?"

"I've already told you the man who could do it. I'm looking at him now."

Clark stood up, eyes wandering over the room, then coming back to the girl who was watching him intently. He couldn't quite make up his mind whether Milly Hayes wanted the Broken Wheel because she thought she had a right to it, being Fred Hayes' cousin, or whether she had other reasons. She was no sentimental fool, Clark would bet on that.

"You're asking me to double-cross Morton?"

"I wouldn't say it that way," Milly said quickly. "Just tell him you've got a better offer. When he sells to me, I'll make you that offer."

"I gave Morton my word. I'm sorry, Miss Hayes."

"A man's got to look out for himself," Milly said softly. "And I've known men who robbed banks. To me there's no difference."

Anger flitted across the girl's even features, but it disappeared instantly behind an impassive mask. "Maybe you had some stake in seeing Fred convicted of a crime he didn't do," she said sharply.

He had expected that from her long before this. "Our decision was based on the evidence given us," he said tightly. "I saw Tom Morton for the first time in my life after the trial this afternoon."

"I'm sorry I said that," Milly said softly, her manner changing like a chameleon's colours. "I'm just disappointed that you don't see things my way. I helped Fred on the ranch with the understanding that some day I would buy a half-interest in it. I can't understand why he should sell to another person without even consulting me."

"If you want to know that, you'll have to ask him," Clark said. "I'm sorry we have to disagree, but there is nothing I can do about it now." He turned away from the window where he had been staring out into the dimly lighted street. "I understand you live in Antelope. That means we'll be neighbours."

She nodded. "I'm postmistress at Antelope. I hope we can be friends." She crossed to the door and turned there, smiling. "I'll be expecting you to call for your mail."

He grinned. "I never let my mail accumulate at the post office."

She was gone then, and he stood staring at the door where she had been. He didn't understand Milly Hayes and her determination to own the Broken Wheel. Probably just an outgrowth of her disappointment. But somehow he doubted if he had heard the last of it.

CHAPTER II

Clark was at the bank in Victor the next morning when it opened. He didn't have to wait for Tom Morton. The rancher greeted him in high spirits.

"Good morning, Hudson," he said cheerily. "I knew you'd be on time. I like a man who is punctual."

"It's a long ride to Porter Valley," Clark said. "And I've got to stop at the Circle C and get my stuff."

"Let's go in and get this straightened up." Morton led the way inside. "How much will you need for your brother's operation?"

"According to my sister's letter, it will take at least six hundred dollars. That's a lot to ask."

Morton shrugged. "I'm not giving it to you. It's just an advance against your share of the profits on the Broken Wheel."

The papers were soon drawn up, and Clark left the bank with a copy of the agreement in his pocket and a bank draft for six hundred dollars ready to mail to his sister.

When the bank draft was mailed, it seemed to Clark that most of his worries had dropped into that letter slot with the letter. It was hard to realize that he had suddenly reached the goal for which he had been struggling for a year.

But on the way to the Circle C, the full meaning of it began to make itself felt. He was tied to Tom Morton and his Broken Wheel. If he valued his word, he would have to stay on the Broken Wheel for at least a year, regardless of the consequences, in order to pay off his obligation to

Morton. Thinking of it now, Clark realized that Morton
had probably counted on Clark honouring that obligation,
come what may. He had seemed almost eager to advance
the money to Clark. There was no better way for Morton
to insure himself against Clark quitting if things started
going against the grain.

Clark nudged his horse along.

He camped that night on Antelope Creek just below
the little settlement of Antelope. He would rather get to
the Broken Wheel in the morning while there was daylight
in which to acquaint himself with the ranch and its
surroundings.

A Nebraska morning in early May can be chilly, and
Clark found it so when he rolled out his blankets. As he
started to pile some buffalo chips for a fire, he noticed the
smoke curling up from the chimneys of Antelope, and a
thought struck him. Why should he fuss over a slow fire
and cook his own breakfast when breakfast was to be had
there in town for a quarter?

He saddled his horse, tied on his bed roll, then rode
into the single street of town. He saw to his disappointment that Antelope was little more than a wide spot in
the trail. There were four or five shacks and a couple of
business houses. But everything was dominated by one big
store building. According to the painting on the false
front, it was the Antelope General Store, selling groceries,
hardware, dry goods, also patent drugs and saddles. Cole
Lardey was proprietor. Below this sign swung a smaller
one proclaiming that also within the building was the
U.S. Post Office.

Clark reined up, whistling softly to himself. Lardey is
Antelope, he thought. What he doesn't run here isn't
worth running.

He looked at the other buildings, but none of them
offered meals. He should have cooked his own breakfast,

he decided. But as long as he was here, he was going to see what the town could offer in the way of a meal.

He rode up to the hitchrack in front of the store and dismounted. Then he went up to the door and tried it only to find it locked.

While he debated what he should do, footsteps crossed the floor inside and halted at the door. Clark waited as the lock slipped back and the door swung open. The man looking out was a medium-sized man but Clark guessed that three or four inches of his height was pushed down into his rounded shoulders. One lock of his sandy hair hung over his pale blue eyes, and he lifted a bony hand to brush it back.

"What do you want?" he demanded, small eyes boring into Clark.

"I was looking for some breakfast," Clark said.

"Beggar!" The man spat the word out contemptuously.

Anger stirred in Clark. "I'm not begging anything. According to the sign, this is a store. I want to buy some grub."

"Ain't time yet for the store to open," the man grumbled. "But come on in. Look around for what you want. I've got some unfinished business to tend to."

The man turned and shuffled off toward the back of the building, and Clark went in, looking along the counter and shelves on the grocery side of the store. He had just gotten a look at the proprietor, Cole Lardey, he guessed, and he couldn't say that he liked what he saw. He wondered how Milly Hayes got along with him. The post office there in the corner would be her domain.

Voices, high-pitched in anger, came from the back room. At first Clark paid no attention, but they soon reached a volume he couldn't ignore.

"You do as I say or I'll flog you within an inch of your

life!" a man yelled, and Clark recognized the voice of the man who had let him in the store.

"That's a sneaking way to fight," a younger voice retorted.

"Don't talk back to me," the older man yelled.

From the back room came the unmistakable sounds of heavy blows, and the youngster cried out. Clark found it hard to stay out of it.

There was a scuffle and more blows. The youngster cried out again, then ran into the store, head down, sobbing. Lardey followed him to the partition door.

"And don't come back till you've finished your job," he yelled.

Lardey went back into the room and the boy slowed to a walk. Seeing Clark suddenly, he wiped a sleeve across his face and stopped, running a critical eye over the stranger.

"You're kind of early, ain't you, mister?" the boy asked.

Clark guessed the lad to be about fourteen or fifteen. He had darker blue eyes than Cole Lardey, and his body was as straight and supple as a whip.

"Not so early when you consider I haven't fed my face yet."

"You're new here. What's your name?"

Clark grinned. Somehow he liked this youngster. "Clark Hudson. I'm taking over the reins on the Broken Wheel. What's your name?"

The boy's mouth formed a small "O". Then he said, "I'm Johnny Lardey. I've got to be shaking off the lice before the old man takes a cane to me."

He went out the front door, and Clark turned back to the counter where he had seen some cheese under the glass. He looked up as someone came through the partition door, but it wasn't Lardey as he expected.

"Good morning, Miss Hayes," he said in surprise. "You didn't waste any time getting back from Victor."

"I might say the same for you," Milly Hayes said. "I had a job to come back to. What's your excuse?"

"Same thing," Clark said. "Running the Broken Wheel. Remember?"

She nodded slowly. "I didn't think you'd be in such a hurry to take over. What will it be for you?"

"I want some of that cheese. But I thought you were the postmistress."

She laughed. "I hand out mail, groceries, hardware, cloth, or whatever you want."

He bought some crackers to go with his cheese and went back outside. He'd have fared better if he'd gone ahead with his own breakfast. But he had learned a little about the town that would have to be his trading centre while he was on the Broken Wheel. He couldn't say that he was favourably impressed.

While he lingered a minute on the porch of the store, he saw two riders coming in on the trail he had just travelled. He waited, feeling no immediate urge to get out to the ranch.

The riders came to the hitchrail in front of the store, and one man dismounted and went around to help the other man down.

"I can make it myself," the man said.

Clark took a closer look at him as he came around the front of his horse, and a shock ran over him. The man was blind. With the help of his companion, the man came up on the porch and moved to the door, feeling his way with a cane.

"This is Cole Lardey's store in Antelope," the guide said.

The blind man nodded. "That's fine, Mr. Skoll." He fished in his pocket and brought out a small handful of gold coins. With his other hand he selected a five-dollar piece. "Here's the money I promised you."

He handed the money to Skoll and turned toward the door. Clark, watching with mild interest, suddenly became alert. Skoll took a coin from his pocket that was almost the size of the gold piece.

"You've made a mistake, Sam," Skoll said. "This is a nickel."

The blind man looked perplexed. "I was sure that was a five-dollar piece."

Skoll held out the nickel he had taken from his own pocket. "Feel it. You can tell it's a nickel."

Clark crossed the porch quickly. "Just a minute, mister. Give him the coin he gave you."

Skoll turned to face Clark, a scowl on his face. "I did."

"You're lying, Skoll. I saw you make the change. He gave you a gold coin."

"This isn't what I gave you," the blind man said, feeling the nickel. "It's too light. I'm sure I didn't make a mistake."

"You didn't," Clark said. "He switched on you."

Skoll grabbed the nickel from the blind man and jammed it into his pocket. "What put-in is it of yours?" he demanded of Clark.

"Anyone who would steal from a blind man is the lowest kind of a skunk," Clark said evenly.

He expected Skoll to take it up, but instead Skoll whirled without a word and went to his horse. The blind man, one shoulder touching the store, spoke in Clark's direction.

"Thanks, mister. I'm grateful to you. But you mustn't saddle yourself with other people's troubles. A man generally has enough of his own."

"I don't cotton to a thief," Clark said.

Cole Lardey came to the door of the store. The frown

that Clark decided was a part of the man was heavy on his face. "What's going on here?"

The blind man turned toward Lardey. "Are you Mr. Lardey?"

"Yeah. Who are you? What do you want?"

"I'm Sam Nixon. I'm looking for the hotel in town."

"There ain't no hotel," Lardey snapped. "And this town don't have room for beggars."

"Oh, I'll pay for my keep," Nixon said quickly, digging into his pocket and coming up with a handful of gold coins that Clark guessed would count out two or three hundred dollars.

Lardey's eyes brightened and his tone changed. "I've got the only building in town big enough to put up strangers. I reckon I can let you have a bed."

"Fine." The blind man seemed elated. "I can do a lot of work. I'd like to help at something." He turned back toward Clark. "Stop in soon and see me, young man."

"I'll do that," Clark said impulsively, wondering momentarily how Nixon knew he was a young man.

Nixon followed Lardey into the store, feeling his way carefully with his cane. Clark turned into the street to his horse.

He couldn't get the blind man out of his thoughts as he rode along the bank of Spring Creek. Lardey's store sat at the junction of Spring Creek and Antelope Creek. Up Spring Creek three or four miles was the Broken Wheel headquarters. The land over which he rode now was part of the Broken Wheel, according to Tom Morton's description.

He wondered about the blind man, Sam Nixon. Evidently Nixon and Skoll had camped not far from him last night. He was surprised that Skoll hadn't robbed the old man then. Why had Nixon wanted to come to Antelope, anyway? Clark couldn't imagine anything there to attract a blind man. And he didn't like Cole Lardey's greedy eyes when he saw Nixon's money. In fact, now that he thought of it, he didn't like Cole Lardey at all.

Off to his left, Clark noticed a row of posts. That would be the fence that Hayes had been trying to put in and protect, Clark guessed. Somewhere along there he had tangled with Old Jed Porter's nephew and young Porter had been killed.

Clark ran his eye up the valley where it sloped up and away from Spring Creek. It was a good valley, but he couldn't understand why Old Jed Porter, being the first man here, had chosen that high dry plateau for a home site when he could have built down here by the spring.

Ahead he saw a grove of trees, an oddity in this country, even along the creeks. In those trees would be the Broken Wheel buildings. Hayes had planted the trees, they said, when he first came to the valley, and they had grown fast as only cottonwoods can. Now they were fifteen to twenty feet high, swaying in the brisk wind.

As he came in sight of the house he saw a small man dart out and leap into the saddle of a waiting horse. Clark used his spurs. A man in that big hurry was up to no good.

But the little man had too long a lead and was a masterful rider, getting the utmost out of his horse. Clark circled the trees and tried to cut down that lead, but he soon saw the futility of it. He checked his horse and went back.

Dismounting in front of the little house, he went inside. His sensitive nostrils caught the odour of kerosene before he got through the door. Looking around quickly, he found the oil-soaked rags piled in two corners of the main room. If he had been two minutes later, the firebug would have had time to set the rags ablaze and he would have been without a house to live in.

He checked over the house, finding some of the furniture broken. At the barn, he found the mangers splintered by an axe. Grimly he went back into the yard. Jed Porter hadn't wasted any time going to work on the Broken Wheel. Clark had heard talk in Victor that Porter had bragged that the Broken Wheel would soon be out of Porter Valley. Clark's jaw set. He had a job now, a job that promised to be the best paying job he'd ever had. And Jed Porter wasn't going to take it away from him.

He went to his horse and got his bedroll, taking it into the house. He was busy trying to make the main room of the house livable when he felt the presence of another person. His hand crept along his belt to his gun as he turned slowly.

"Don't get itchy fingers, Mister."

Clark jerked his hand away from his gun as if he'd been burned. That was a girl's voice, and one glance at her in the doorway proved that she didn't even have a gun.

"I wasn't expecting company," Clark said by way of apology.

"You won't have much if that's the way you're going to welcome people."

Clark looked around for a chair that wasn't splintered to offer to the girl. She still stood in the doorway, a straight-backed slender girl, nearly a foot shorter than Clark. Her hat was pushed back a little off her blonde hair, and her eyes were the clearest blue Clark had ever seen. Her shirt was open at the throat, and her denim riding pants were tucked into small boots.

Clark found a chair that had the back broken off but otherwise was durable. "Come in and sit down," he said, pulling the chair around. "Somebody was a little reckless with the furniture."

"You won't want me to stay when you find out who I am," the girl said, still not moving from the doorway. "I'm Linda Porter, Jed Porter's niece."

Clark wasn't too surprised. He had heard that Luke Porter, the man Fred Hayes had been convicted of murdering, had a sister, but she hadn't appeared at the trial.

"You're still welcome to come in and sit down," Clark said. "I doubt if we're destined to be the best of friends, considering the situation, but we don't have to declare war on sight."

A trace of a smile touched her lips, and she came into the room. "Maybe not. Why did you buy into this mess?"

"It's a good paying job. Nothing wrong with taking a good job, is there?"

"It's your gun Tom Morton hired. You know that."

"Well, I didn't leave my gun behind, it's true. But I hope I don't have to use it here. There's room for two ranches in this valley."

"Not if one of them controls all the water. Uncle Jed thought there was room for him and the nesters that settled along this creek. But when they tried fencing off the water, that meant war."

"Morton didn't say anything about fencing off the water now."

"Uncle Jed is through taking chances. He gave Fred Hayes an inch and he took a mile. He won't tolerate any ranch here now."

Clark moved across the cluttered room to the window and looked out into the trees. This was a pretty place, he thought. He wondered why Fred Hayes had risked losing it just to shut Porter off from water.

"Just how does he figure on running Morton out of the valley?" he asked.

"Uncle Jed is a fighting man. He tried to live here in peace. You can see what it got him. You figure out what he's liable to do now."

Clark sighed. It didn't take much figuring. "Can't he

dig wells up the valley? Then it wouldn't make any difference to him what Morton did with the creek."

Linda Porter got off the broken chair and went to the door. There she turned, speaking with the patience of one explaining a simple thing to a child.

"He can dig wells. But he's got almost two thousand cattle. Did you ever stop to think how much water it would take for that many thirsty cattle during August?"

Clark nodded slowly. "It would take several wells and windmills, I reckon. So far as I'm concerned, he can water his stuff here in Spring Creek."

"He'll do that with or without your consent. But he'll never trust another neighbour here."

Suddenly an idea struck Clark. He looked at Linda standing by the door and the idea grew into a suspicion. She would look very much like a small man if she were bending low over a running horse.

"Is this your second visit here this morning?" he asked, his eyes wandering to the piles of kerosene-soaked rags that he hadn't had time to remove.

"No." A slight frown tugged at her forehead. "We heard that Morton was putting somebody on the Broken Wheel. When I saw you here this morning, I rode down to see what kind of a gunman he had sent."

"You figured it would be a gunman?"

"Uncle Jed knows Tom Morton. He's expecting trouble. But what made you think I'd been here before?"

"Somebody tried to burn the house." He nodded to the rags in the corner.

Linda looked and laughed. "If I'd gotten that far, I'd have finished it. In fact, if that was my work, I'd throw a match in it right now. But I don't even have a match with me."

Looking at the girl, Clark didn't doubt that she might do just that. But if she hadn't been the firebug, it must have been one of the Walking L men. Linda Porter probably knew something about it.

"How many men are working on the Walking L?" Clark asked.

"Enough to push you out of here," Linda said easily. "Uncle Jed or Sid Bodey, our foreman, will probably be down to see you as soon as I tell them you're here."

"They probably know it by now," Clark said, thinking of the man who had ridden away in such a hurry when he came in this morning. "If your uncle needed this water so bad, why didn't he build here? He had the valley all to himself, didn't he?"

Linda sighed as if the subject were a sore spot. "He had the whole west end of the state, almost," she said. "He wanted to be up there where he could look over the whole valley. It was his world. He wouldn't consider the fact that some day there would be other people here."

There was irritation in her voice, and it was the first indication to Clark that everything was not in accord up at the Walking L.

"Can't he see now that if he runs me out, somebody else will take my place?"

Linda shook her head, a blonde curl swinging across her forehead. "All he can see is that you're taking the water he thinks is rightfully his. I can't say that I blame him. He tried being neighbourly with Fred Hayes. Now he thinks the only way to hold this valley is with force. And if you knew Jed Porter, you'd know that means trouble."

"I can imagine," Clark said, remembering the man as he had been in the courtroom in Victor during the trial of Fred Hayes. He was a thin man, over six feet tall and still not stooped, with iron grey hair that showed no signs of thinning and piercing blue eyes. He'd be a tough man to handle, Clark decided.

Linda stepped into the doorway. "I know I'd be wasting my breath to tell you to pull out of this."

Clark nodded. "I reckon you would."

She turned without another word and crossed the yard to her buckskin pony. Mounting, she reined him up the slope to the west.

Clark stood in the doorway and watched her go. A pretty girl, he thought, with plenty of spunk. And, he added bitterly, practically looking over a gunsight at him right now.

CHAPTER III

Although Clark set himself for a stormy visit from Jed Porter, he saw nothing of the old man that day. It gave him time to look over the house and barn on the Broken Wheel.

The first inspection of the house led him to a startling discovery. In one of the two small back rooms his attention was caught by the sound of running water. A quick investigation showed him that the room had been built over the edge of the big spring. A trap door lifted out of the floor in the corner of the room above the water. A bucket could be lowered through the hole and clean fresh water pulled up into the house.

Outside, Clark inspected the back of the house and found it built on stilts a couple of feet above the level of the water that gushed out to flow down the crooked stream. Clark wondered why Hayes hadn't built his house a few feet from the spring. It certainly wasn't because he couldn't find a level space.

Clark spread his bedroll on the bed in the little room above the spring that night, and the gurgling water beneath quickly lulled him to sleep.

It wasn't until mid-forenoon the next day that the expected visit from Porter came. Clark had straightened up the house, carrying out the broken furniture and mending what could be salvaged. Morton had picked him for a gunman, but this morning he felt more like a housewife.

Porter, tall and straight in the saddle as if he had a ramrod lashed to his back, rode up to the front of the house.

A heavy-set man, several inches shorter than Porter, rode beside him and swung down with the tall thin man to wait for Clark to come out of the house.

Clark, looking through the window, noticed that both men wore guns. But it was habitual with them, and Clark put no special significance on it. Buckling on his own gun belt, he went outside.

"Howdy, Porter," he said. "I had a notion you'd be over to see me before long."

Porter's face was long and thin. The years of bright sunlight had driven his eyes back into his head but it hadn't dimmed the fire in them.

"You know why I'm here, Hudson," he said in his high-pitched voice. "I trusted one neighbour. He tried to ruin me and finally killed my nephew. There ain't room in this valley for anybody but the Walking L."

"Pull in your horns a little, Porter, and there will be room," Clark said calmly. "I'm not figuring on crowding you. As far as I'm concerned, you can water at the creek."

Porter pushed out his chest. "Hayes told me the same thing. Then he fenced me off. Nobody else is going to get such a foothold in this valley. I'm giving you plenty warning. Just pack up and get out."

Clark shifted over to stand by one of the trees, convinced that there was to be no gun trouble this morning. "I've got a job here, Porter. When Tom Morton tells me to get out, I'll do it. But I'm taking orders from him."

The heavy man, less than half Porter's age, moved forward a step, his face twisted in a scowl. "Morton's a long ways from here, Hudson. He won't come running when you howl. You can find lots healthier jobs than this one."

"I'm keeping in pretty good health. And I like my job."

"That could change mighty fast," the heavy man snapped.

"Shut up, Sid," Porter said, running a hand thoughtfully over his moustache. "I won't give you an inch, Hudson. I'm watering my cattle at the creek where they ought to water. The first sign of interference you show, and you'll have the biggest fight on your hands you've ever seen."

Clark nodded. "Morton hasn't said a word about trying to rebuild the fence Hayes had."

"He'd better not," Porter said, and swung easily back into the saddle. "If he does, you'd better talk him out of it or look for another job. This one sure won't be healthy. Come on, Sid."

Clark watched them ride away. He had placed the short man now. He must be Sid Bodey, Porter's foreman. Linda had said he would probably be over to pay him a visit. Clark had a feeling Milly Hayes hadn't been too far wrong when she predicted there would be blood on the grass here in Porter Valley before this was all settled. Porter had his head set on clearing the valley of the Broken Wheel. And Tom Morton was a stubborn man. Clark was caught in the middle, bound by honour to pay Morton the debt he owed. Facing down the Walking L evidently was going to be the way he would have to pay that debt.

Clark saddled his horse and rode down the creek to Antelope. He didn't know how often the mail got in, but he aimed to keep a watch on it, for Morton might use the mail to send him instructions.

The hitchrack in front of Lardey's store was empty when Clark rode up, and he found the inside of the store the same. A cowbell, hanging so that the door struck it when it opened, clanged noisily. Clark waited a minute before Johnny Lardey came through the back door.

"Howdy, Mr. Hudson," Johnny said, moving in behind a counter. "What will it be for you?"

"I just came in to call for my mail. Where's Miss Hayes?"

Johnny shrugged. "Probably back in the kitchen or her room. She's always here when the mail comes in, which is three times a week, but the rest of the time, there's no telling where she might be. I'll see if you've got any mail."

He went into the post office section and thumbed through a little pile of letters. "Nothing for you," he said.

Clark went out on the porch. He should be hearing from Tom Morton soon. Probably Morton would be up in person, he decided.

Mounting his horse, he reined up the dusty road that served as a street. As he was passing the last shack between him and the open prairie, his eye caught the huddled form of a man lying against the side of the shack. Clark reined his horse over and swung down.

At first glance he thought the man was dead. But then a shudder ran over the man and Clark recognized Sam Nixon, the blind man who had rented a room from Lardey. He knelt beside Nixon and examined him quickly. A lump on his head seemed to be the extent of his injuries.

While Clark worked over Nixon, the blind man regained consciousness and sat up. He felt around for his cane, found it, and was going to get to his feet, but Clark held him down.

"Better take it easy for a little while, Nixon. You got a bad bump on the noggin. What did you hit?"

"I didn't hit a thing," Nixon said. "But something sure hit me." He rubbed a hand gently over his head then ran his fingers down over his pockets. Despair washed over his face. "They got my money," he moaned.

Clark frowned. "Everything you had?"

Nixon nodded. "Every bit of it. The only place I can keep it where somebody can't steal it is right in my pockets." He shook his head sadly. "That isn't even a safe place." He ran his hand over his coat pockets. "They cleaned out my letters and everything. Some people are greedier than a hungry pig."

"Do you have any idea who it was?"

"No. They were mighty careful not to say anything; at least, not until they had cracked me over the head. But I'll know them if I ever hear them run."

"How many were there?" Clark asked, wondering how much the old man had learned through his hearing.

"Two. And one of them was about as graceful at running as an elephant in a cracker barrel."

Clark couldn't help marvelling at the blind man. Despair had been keen in the old fellow when he discovered he had been robbed, but already that despair was fading.

Clark helped Nixon to his feet. "What are you going to do now?"

"Get a job somewhere. I can work all right. There are other ways of seeing than with your eyes."

Clark watched the blind man as he felt his way out into the street with the cane. He pitied the man, yet there was something about him that left no room for pity.

"Just how do you see things, Nixon?"

Nixon lifted the cane. "According to what it is. If it's something that doesn't move, I see it with this cane. If it's something that moves and makes a noise, I use my ears. Now I've never seen you the way you think of seeing things, but I know pretty well what you look like."

Clark's interest in this man was growing. "How would you describe me?"

"I'd say you are an inch or two over six feet."

"What makes you think so?"

"Well, your voice doesn't come out of the top of your head and it's above the level of my head." Nixon smiled. "If you had your eyes closed for a year or two you'd learn to let your ears see for you. Judging from your walk, I'd say you tipped the scales close to two hundred pounds. You're not the size of a fellow I'd pick for a rough and tumble fight even if I had my eyes."

Nixon's accurate description of his size made Clark look at the blind man in a new light. A man who was as observant as Nixon wouldn't be much of a handicap to have around even without his sight. Clark began toying with an idea that had struck him.

"Are you figuring on staying in Antelope now?" he asked.

Nixon shrugged. "Nothing else I can do, I guess. I'll find somebody who will give me a little work. It doesn't take much money for me to live on."

"Ever been on a ranch?"

"Born and raised on a ranch. Lived there until I lost my sight. You wouldn't be hinting that I might be of some use to you on your ranch, would you?"

Clark grinned. "I was kicking the idea around."

Eagerness spread over Nixon's face. "I can do most of the house work. I can cook, too, if you'll show me where things are in the kitchen, then let me do all the work there so nothing gets changed around. You're not married, are you?"

"Nope. And no prospects."

"I can save you a lot of time by doing the chores and the cooking."

Clark was sceptical about the cooking. But he didn't doubt that Nixon could do a lot of the tedious chores. Clark would not only be giving the old fellow a home, but he'd have some company for himself, too.

"Let's get your horse," he said. "We'll see how handy you are at doing chores."

Before he left the spot, Clark checked the area carefully for some sign left by the robbers, but he found nothing.

He went after Nixon's horse while the blind man headed toward Lardey's for his suitcase. Clark watched him go along the street with almost as much confidence as a man with eyes. When he brought the horse to the store, Nixon was waiting on the porch.

At the Broken Wheel, Nixon insisted on going to the barn with Clark to put the horses away.

"I might want to know where the barn and the horses are some time," he explained.

In the house, he moved from room to room, feeling his way cautiously with his cane. He asked innumerable questions and went over the kitchen with tedious thoroughness, having Clark identify the contents of every can and box.

"I can cook a meal for you now," he said when they finished. "But you'd feel safer if you watched me do it for the first time."

"You can't remember what's in all those cans," Clark said dubiously.

Nixon grinned. "I'd bet with you but I don't like to take your money. You watch me get supper and see if I get hold of the wrong can."

Clark might have put him to the test right then, but the sound of hoofbeats drifted into the house. He turned through the door and waited, watching the approaching riders through the low branches of a tree. He recognized one man as Tom Morton and stepped out into the yard to meet him.

Morton raised a hand in greeting as he pulled his horse to a stop. The rider beside him reined up and dismounted when Morton did.

"I see you got here in time to keep the place intact," Morton said, glancing around.

"If I'd been ten minutes later, it would have gone up in smoke."

Morton nodded, showing no surprise. "I figured they'd try something like that as soon as they found out I'd bought it. Glad you got here in time. What kind of shape is the fence in that Hayes built?"

"It's down," Clark said. "And it had better stay down unless you want a shooting war with Jed Porter."

Morton's eyes narrowed. "Porter doesn't own the Broken Wheel."

"The creek is the only place where he can water his cattle," Clark said.

"I'll be fair with him. He can still water at the creek if he'll build a lane from his land to the creek and keep up the fence so his cattle don't get through."

Clark shook his head, remembering what Linda had said about Porter never trusting another neighbour. "He won't do it. The day we start stringing wire, he'll start throwing lead."

Morton paced the yard angrily. "What does he expect me to do? After all, I own this ranch. I could fence it off tight so he couldn't get a drop of water. He ought to jump at the chance I'm offering. You tell him my proposition and see if he turns it down."

"I'm betting he will. Why does the fence have to be put up?"

"I'm bringing in a herd of purebred whiteface cattle. There's money in Herefords. I don't want the calves mixed with that longhorn stuff."

Clark shook his head slowly. There wasn't room in Porter Valley for Herefords and longhorns. He knew it. And Morton ought to know it, too.

"That's asking for trouble, don't you think?" he said.

Morton shook his head. "I'm after profits. You ought to be, too. One fat whiteface will bring more money than two skinny longhorns. And you never saw a longhorn that wasn't skinny. The money is in the whitefaces and I aim to get some of it."

"That sounds good," Clark admitted. "But Herefords aren't immune to bullets. And neither am I. You don't expect me to work this place alone, do you?"

"Of course not. As soon as you get the fence fixed around this little pasture close to the house, I'll bring the herd. And I'll bring along two or three men to work for you. I want you to fix the fence all the way to Antelope. Most of the fence is already there. It's down, I know. But it shouldn't be too much work to stretch it up again."

Clark squinted his eyes out over the rich grass along the creek, tall enough now to wave a little in the breeze. "Stretching the wire will be the little end of the job."

"There's money in Herefords," Morton reminded him.

"I know that," Clark said. "There's money in funerals, too, if you're an undertaker."

"Don't you think you can do it?"

Clark answered slowly. "A man never knows what he can do till he tries."

Nixon came to the door of the house and stopped. Morton jerked his head toward Nixon and spoke in a low tone.

"What's that?"

"He's my flunkey," Clark explained.

Morton frowned and shook his head. "He's blind."

"I can see as much as you can," Nixon said suddenly from the doorway.

Morton started, and Clark found it hard to believe that Nixon could have overheard the rancher's low tones.

"Perhaps I was mistaken," Morton said in confusion. "I thought you couldn't see."

"I don't see with my eyes," Nixon said, feeling his way into the yard with his cane. "But if anything happens, I'll know about it. You don't need to worry about your place here. I'll hold it down while Clark is herding Porter's outfit away."

"That's good," Morton said dubiously, and looked at Clark. "How about it?"

"I'll start on the pasture fence right away. But I won't tackle that down toward Antelope until you send up some help. When will you have the herd here?"

"In about a week. That ought to give you plenty of time to get this little pasture fixed."

"I'll have it ready," Clark promised.

Morton and the man with him mounted, and Clark watched them ride out of the yard.

"That man loves a dollar," Nixon said at Clark's elbow.

Clark nodded. "Bringing whitefaces in here may mean trouble."

"With Jed Porter sitting in the upper end of this valley, it will mean trouble," Nixon said with finality.

Clark looked quickly at Nixon. "Do you know Porter?"

Nixon smiled wisely. "Slightly," he said, and turned toward the house. "Just slightly."

Clark watched him go, his cane mapping a path ahead of him. Slightly, the way Nixon had said it, meant a lot. Sam Nixon knew more than he was telling.

CHAPTER IV

Clark found fence-building tools in the barn where Fred Hayes had evidently left them. The fence was in worse shape than he had expected, the wire being cut between many of the posts and the posts broken off. It was a good job of destruction.

Clark pulled the staples out of the posts, freeing the wire, then began resetting the posts, keeping in sight of the house through the morning. He had a feeling that the place was being watched, and he didn't like the idea of leaving Nixon alone. Nixon had proved that he could take care of himself as long as there was no outside interference. He had cooked supper the night before with Clark hovering over him, and he hadn't made a mistake. He was getting the feel of his surroundings and he had already taken over much of the housework. Clark knew that he hadn't made a mistake in taking in Sam Nixon.

He had reset a dozen or fifteen posts when the callers he had been expecting from the Walking L came. Jed Porter wasn't in the group that rode down over the hill and pulled up where Clark was digging a post hole. The only man Clark recognized was Porter's foreman, Sid Bodey.

"Changed your mind pretty fast, didn't you?" Bodey said, leaning over his saddle horn in feigned relaxation. "You said yesterday you didn't aim to rebuild this fence."

Clark stopped his digging. "I work on orders the same as you, Bodey. Morton aims to bring in some cattle and he wants this little pasture fenced in."

"What comes after the little pasture?" Bodey asked

darkly. "The rest of the creek all the way to Antelope?"

"Maybe. But Morton said he'd leave a lane for Walking L cattle to get to water if you'd keep up the fence in that lane."

"Now isn't that generous of him?" Bodey snapped, his scowl deepening. "We'll water at the creek, all right, but the only fence we'll fix will be with wire clippers."

"Don't be too sure of that Bodey," Clark said, the man's arrogance working under his skin.

"Who's going to stop us?"

Clark frowned. "I've done bigger jobs myself."

Bodey leaned farther over his saddle. "It was right about here that Hayes shot Old Jed's nephew. Maybe you'd like to try something like that now."

Clark jammed his diggers into the ground and walked over close to the Walking L foreman. "Listen, Bodey. I'm here on a job and I aim to do it. As long as you tend to your own business, we'll get along. But I'm not a man who'll take too much riding. Now you'd better take your gun-happy boys back to Jed Porter and tell him to talk to Tom Morton. After he's talked to Morton, he'll know enough about what's going on to give you some orders."

But Bodey only bristled. With three men backing him, he was pushing for a showdown that could go only one way.

"You talk mighty big, Hudson. Do you act as big as you talk?"

"That's according to whether I have anything big to act on. Right now I haven't."

Bodey's neck and face burned red. There was a movement behind him and one man let a grin flit across his face. Bodey twisted to look at the men. Apparently he didn't see the backing he needed to push this thing any farther.

"I'm giving you fair warning, Hudson," he blustered.

"When the Walking L cattle want water, they're going to the creek by the shortest route. If your fence is in the way, it's just too bad."

The Walking L foreman wheeled his horse and pounded over the hill, his three men following him. Clark, still frowning, turned back to his work.

The sun got hotter, and it seemed to Clark that the ground got harder. He stopped for a rest, moving over into the shade of the bluff that bordered the creek. Sitting there, he could see upstream to the Broken Wheel buildings and downstream for nearly a mile.

He took off his hat and ran his bandana over his forehead. It was then, with his head bowed, that he caught the glint of the sun on a little piece of metal almost hidden in the new grass. Reaching over, he picked it up, and in a second his mind was racing wildly on a theory that had stuck in the back of his mind since Fred Hayes' trial.

It was an empty rifle cartridge he held in his hand. Clark glanced down along the fence to the spot where Bodey had said young Porter had been killed. It wasn't more than a hundred yards from the spot where he was sitting now. At the trial Fred Hayes had insisted that he had been at his house when he heard the shot that killed Luke Porter. He had investigated, and so had Jed Porter and some of his men who had been holding cattle back, waiting for Luke to cut the wires so they could water the stock. Porter and his men had found Hayes standing over Luke's body. In view of the previous quarrels and Hayes' threats to any and all Walking L riders, Hayes had been convicted. Now Clark's faint doubts had suddenly come alive.

Clark examined the empty shell closer. It hadn't been fired from a Winchester .44 such as he carried and such as most other saddle men here carried. It was a little bigger than the .44 and had come from a rim fire rifle. A Spencer .56, he'd guess.

Finding the empty shell here in this secluded nook in the bluff didn't prove that somebody other than Fred Hayes had done the killing. Hayes might have done it from this very nook in order to divert suspicion from him, but it hardly seemed likely that he would let himself be found with the body afterward. And it could easily be that this cartridge had been fired at something other than a man. But in Clark's mind, the theory that he had considered before was almost a certainty now. Somebody else had wanted Luke Porter out of the way. Who and why were questions that would have to wait for another day for their answer.

Clark dropped the empty cylinder in his pocket and went back to his work. When he returned to the house at noon he found dinner waiting and Nixon in high spirits, anticipating Clark's approval of the meal. Clark didn't disappoint him.

A rider came into the yard before Clark was ready to go back to his fence building. He waved a welcome as Milly Hayes swung down and came across the yard to the door.

"Come on in," Clark invited, "I didn't expect to see you out here."

Milly laughed lightly, "Remember I told you once that you never know what to expect of me."

"Seems I'm a little slow learning," Clark said, grinning.

"No mail today," Milly said, "and I felt like riding. I thought I'd drop by and see how Mr. Nixon got over his bump. Cole was telling me about it."

"I'm still in one piece," Nixon said, and Clark noticed the edge on his voice. "But no thanks to anyone in Antelope."

"I'm sorry I wasn't there, Mr. Nixon," Milly said

amiably. "I would have been glad to have taken care of you."

"I'd rather take care of myself," Nixon said, and went into the kitchen, his cane thumping the floor ahead of him.

Milly frowned. "Who twisted his tail?"

"I don't know," Clark said. "Maybe his dinner didn't agree with him."

"Could be that wallop on his head."

"Maybe. But he hasn't shown any ill effects before."

Milly laughed. "Guess I just rubbed him wrong. I've got to get back. I promised Cole I'd watch the store for him this afternoon. Why don't you come down once in a while? It gets lonesome."

"I'm pretty busy now," Clark said. "But I'll be in after my mail once in a while. Drop in again when you're out riding."

"I will." Milly went through the door. "This is just a nice ride from town. And I'm interested in how you make out against the Walking L."

Clark watched her mount and ride down the creek. He wondered why she had come. It wasn't because of concern over Sam Nixon. Maybe, as she had said, she was just lonesome. That sounded logical to Clark. Wouldn't be a bad job cheering her up, he thought as he turned back into the house.

"Think she's pretty nice, don't you?" Nixon said from the partition doorway.

Clark looked sharply at the blind man. "What makes you say that?"

"I can see some things better without eyes."

"Well," Clark admitted, "maybe you're right. She does seem pretty nice. Any objections?"

"Plenty," Nixon said sharply. "But it wouldn't do me any good to make them. I remember the first time I saw a locoweed. It was in bloom and I thought it was a mighty pretty little plant."

"You mean you haven't always been blind?"

Nixon shook his head. "No. Once I could see as well as you. And all I could see then was the outside of things. I got a good dose of locoweed, too."

Nixon went back into the kitchen, and Clark turned toward his work on the pasture fence. He wondered what Nixon knew about Milly Hayes. Maybe he had just taken a dislike to her. But Clark preferred to think there was something else behind his antagonism. There was more to the man than first met the eye.

Clark and Nixon had fixed up the room that was built over the spring for their bedroom. Dog tired when he finished his day's work on the fence, Clark went to bed soon after supper. The gurgling water under the floor lulled him to sleep immediately.

He was deep in sleep when he felt something shaking him. He fought his way back to full consciousness and sat up. It was dark in the little room, but he could make out Nixon standing by his bed.

"Are you dead?" Nixon whispered.

"What's wrong?" Clark asked, keeping his voice low.

"We've got company."

Clark listened carefully, but he didn't hear a sound other than the gurgling water. "I don't hear anything."

"That doesn't mean there's nothing to hear," Nixon said. "There are several riders outside. I heard them come. They're trying to be quiet. That means mischief. Better get your guns handy and give me one. I can't see what I'm shooting at, but there won't be anything out there that I don't want to hit. I might be lucky."

Reluctantly, Clark got out of bed. It seemed fantastic that anyone could hear a sound outside, but already he had learned not to question Nixon's uncanny hearing.

Moving into the next room, he got a rifle and handed it to Nixon while he got his own six-gun.

There, away from the gurgling water and with everything quiet in the room, Clark heard the movements outside. Gliding to the window, he peered out. There was no moon, but the light from the stars was enough to show several riderless horses standing in a cluster at the corner of the barn.

"You're right, Sam," Clark whispered to the blind man at his elbow. "We've got company and they don't want us to know it."

"Of course I'm right," Nixon said indignantly. "Now be quiet a minute. I'll find out what they're up to."

For a long minute, Clark almost held his breath. He caught one or two faint rustling sounds but he could neither distinguish nor locate them. But Nixon apparently did both.

"They're piling stuff against the side of the house over there," he whispered, and pointed across the room. "They just poured something on. Must be kerosene. What are we waiting for?"

Crossing quickly to the door, Clark threw it open and stepped back. "What do you want out there?" he yelled.

His answer was a volley of bullets. Two men ran from the corner of the house and Nixon leaped toward the door.

"Jed Porter," he yelled. "I know his run." He lifted the rifle and fired toward the fleeing men.

More shots snapped through the door and the far wall. Clark pulled Nixon down out of the doorway and opened fire with his .45. The bobbing figures in the gloom were hard to get over his sights, but he saw one man stumble and the other man stop to lend him an arm.

Within a minute, the raiders were gone. Clark had expected them to make a stand at the barn and finish the job they had started. But apparently all they had wanted to do was burn him out, not kill him. When the horses had pounded up over the hill, Nixon heaved a sigh and set the rifle down.

"Did I hit anything?"

"One of us did," Clark said. "Didn't kill him, but we made him wish he'd stayed at home tonight."

"Was it Porter?"

"Couldn't tell," Clark admitted. "But I think it was a short man. Porter is tall."

"You don't have to tell me what Porter looks like," Nixon said, and turned toward the bedroom. "Well, let's finish our sleep. Maybe you ought to see what damage they did. I wouldn't be much good at that."

Clark, still carrying his gun, went outside. He had learned long ago never to trust an enemy, especially a sneak enemy such as the one who had struck tonight. He had seen a gang of raiders run one night. But behind they had left an ambush. When the defenders relaxed, the trap was sprung.

Outside, Clark studied the yard carefully before venturing around the house where Nixon said they had been piling stuff. He found it just as Nixon said it would be. Rags and sticks piled against the house and the smell of kerosene was strong in the air. Again he had been just in the nick of time to keep from being burned out. This time he had Nixon to thank for it. If he had been alone in the house, he wouldn't have wakened until the flames were out of control.

He kicked the rags and sticks away from the house, wondering if Nixon were right in naming the raiders. He couldn't doubt the blind man. He had been right in almost everything else. Apparently he knew Jed Porter pretty well to be able to recognize his run.

Again he thought of Milly Hayes and wondered how she fitted into things and what Nixon really knew about her. Back in the house, he found Nixon still awake and decided that this would be a good time to find out how much Nixon could and would tell.

"Tried to burn us out, all right," Clark said. "But how did you know it was Porter's outfit?"

"I told you I know the way he runs," Nixon said. "He limps when he runs. Anyway, who else would want to burn you out? And you said there were several horses. Who else around here has that big an outfit?"

Clark nodded. "It seems to point straight at the Walking L, all right. Does Milly Hayes fit into this mix-up anywhere?"

Nixon was quiet for a while. "Fred Hayes was her cousin," he said finally, and Clark felt that he was stalling. "I don't imagine there is any love lost between her and the Walking L."

"Think she'd like to join me in fighting Porter?"

"Maybe," said Nixon slowly. "But only if the winner is going to be Milly Hayes."

"You know a lot you're not telling me," Clark accused.

"Could be," Nixon admitted. "But I've learned that the noisiest birds are generally the most disliked."

Nixon turned his face to the wall and settled his head in his pillow.

CHAPTER V

It had been a long night for Linda Porter. She had heard her uncle and the men ride away shortly before midnight. Ten men riding out at that hour meant trouble. She was sure she knew where they were going. But she could only guess what they were going to do. There would probably be a fight. And somebody was likely to get hurt.

She heard the men come back sometime after two o'clock. There was talking, loud and vehement, down in the yard, but she couldn't understand any of it. Anyway, it was none of her business. Her uncle had told her hundreds of times that women were meant to be seen and not heard and never should they interfere with men's work.

At breakfast, she waited for Jed Porter to mention last night's escapade, but he held a rigid silence. Apparently things hadn't gone as had been expected. Linda had resigned herself to a gnawing curiosity when one of the Walking L riders knocked on the front door. Linda opened it.

"The boss here?" he asked.

She nodded. "Of course. He's eating breakfast. Is it important?"

Linda knew how Jed hated to be interrupted at his meals. There was a time and place for everything, according to Jed. And mealtime was neither the time nor place for business.

"It sure is important," the man said.

Linda stepped back and let the rider in. He went directly to the table.

"What's wrong, Rusty?" Jed demanded irritably.

"Looks like we're going to have to get a doc for Sid," Rusty said.

Jed kicked back his chair and strode angrily around the room. "And let the whole world know we were the ones who made that raid last night?"

"I reckon everybody will guess anyway," Rusty said. "Sid ain't doing so good. His arm's purple clear to his shoulder."

Linda, watching Jed Porter pace the room, couldn't remember seeing him look so thin and haggard. King of Porter Valley less than two years ago, now he was fighting for his very existence. And Linda wondered if it wasn't a losing fight. Jed ran a bony hand through his thick curly grey hair and paced some more. But still he didn't give permission to go for a doctor.

"Uncle Jed," Linda began timidly, knowing how Jed hated interruptions and yet feeling that she could give the kind of help he needed.

"This is none of your affair, Linda," Jed snapped, and continued his pacing.

"You sent me away to school," Linda said bravely. "I learned a few things there that can help you now."

Jed snorted. "What good will book learning do? Did they teach you how to make water spring up on a dry hill so I can water my cattle?"

Linda's chin came up. "No. But they taught me how to care for wounds. Maybe I can fix Sid's arm so you won't need a doctor."

Jed's face held its rigid lines. "That's no job for a girl. It takes a man to handle things like that."

Rusty bit his lip, then blurted out his opposition to Porter. "Give her a chance, boss. Sid's got to have something done. And none of us down at the bunkhouse know what to do. If you won't get a doc, let Linda try. We can't lose nothing."

Jed turned a heavy scowl on the cowboy but said nothing. He ran his hand through his hair again and down over his face. "All right," he said finally as though admitting a major defeat. "Bring Sid up here and let her work on him."

Jed left his breakfast and went into his room. Linda hurried to the kitchen and put the old iron teakettle on the front of the stove, filled it with water, and stuffed in all the chips the stove would hold.

Sid Bodey came to the house, helped by Rusty and another puncher, walking under his own power but looking weak and unsteady on his feet. Linda motioned him into the kitchen, set him on a chair, and went to work.

The wound wasn't such a bad one but it hadn't had any care. Infection was setting in, and Linda found her work cut out for her. If it got out of hand, gangrene could set in and the foreman would lose an arm or maybe his life.

"Didn't think Jed would let you do anything like this," Bodey said as she gently washed the arm.

"It wasn't his idea," Linda admitted. "How did this happen?"

"I got on the wrong end of a bullet," Bodey said evasively.

Linda looked at the foreman's face. His feelings were written there for her to read. He was grateful to her for dressing his wound but he didn't want to answer questions. He was afraid of Jed Porter. Every man in the Walking L crew was afraid of Jed.

"Did this bullet have Clark Hudson's brand on it?" Linda asked softly.

Bodey hesitated. "It wasn't General Custer's," he mumbled finally.

"Burn him out?" Linda pressed.

"Naw. He heard us. He could hear a pin drop in a boiler factory."

Somehow that news was heartening to Linda. She wanted Jed to hold the valley, for she felt it belonged to him. He had been here first and had worked hard to make a home here. He had been like a father to her brother, Luke, and had sent her East for an education. She owed him her loyalty, at least. But she didn't want to see him go outside the law to hold the valley.

She finished dressing Bodey's arm and was satisfied with the job she had done. "I don't think you'll have to get a doctor for that now, Sid. Just be careful to keep every bit of dirt away from it and don't use it. Come back at noon and let me dress it again."

Bodey grinned weakly. "Thanks, Linda. Maybe you can get me fixed up so I can go back and blast that gunslick off the earth."

He left the house and Linda watched him go, a sinking feeling inside her. Was she really helping Jed by getting a man such as Sid Bodey back on the active list? He was the kind who would rather work outside the law, it seemed to her.

Bodey's arm improved rapidly, and even Jed had limited praise for Linda. But he had a warning for her, too, a warning that was really aimed at the men on the Walking L payroll.

"As soon as Sid's arm is out of danger, you turn that job of doctoring over to Rusty," Jed ordered. "And stay away from the boys. It cost me the price of fifty head of cattle to educate you, and I'd give that much more if you were as homely as a scarecrow. Instead, you turn every man's head the minute he lays eyes on you. If any Walking L puncher gets mooney over you, he draws his pay right there and then. Women have no place in a man's world."

Linda watched Jed pace the floor as he raved. Women were the sore spot of his life. So far as she knew, Linda was the only woman who had set foot in the Walking L ranchhouse in the last ten years.

"You didn't think so when you were young, did you, Uncle Jed?" she asked, knowing this was the one subject on which he wouldn't argue with her.

"I made a mistake that ruined my life. I won't have another man around who is that foolish. So stay away from the boys who work for me. Understand?"

Linda nodded. "I always have stayed away from them. There is no one on this ranch who would interest me, anyway."

"Make sure they don't get interested in you," Jed warned, and stamped out of the house.

Bodey's arm healed and Linda settled back into her routine of housework and daily horseback rides. But that routine was thrown into confusion when Jed stormed into the house while she was getting breakfast one morning, his face livid with rage.

Linda turned from the stove. "What's wrong, Uncle Jed?"

"Somebody stole ten of my best horses!" Jed roared.

Linda looked through the window to the corrals. "Out of the corrals?"

"Right out from under our very noses," Jed said, stamping across the room.

"They can't get away with them. You'll know them if you see them."

"If I see them. No horse thief is dumb enough to let me set eyes on those horses again if he can help it."

"Aren't you going after them?"

Jed was already in the living room. "The boys are saddling up now." He lifted a rifle down from its rack.

"What about breakfast?" Linda asked.

"Breakfast be hanged! I'll eat when I've run those varmints down."

"Any idea who did it?"

Jed examined his rifle, then stared fiercely at his niece. "A mighty good idea. Morton wants war. That was plain enough when he hired that gun-slinger, Hudson, to run the Broken Wheel, then started rebuilding that fence. He knew that stealing our horses would cripple us more than anything he could do."

"But didn't he take all your horses?"

"No. But he took the best." Jed picked up the rifle and headed for the door. "We'll get them back, though, if we have to kill every thieving son in the valley."

Linda watched him as he met the riders in the yard and swung up on his horse. Suddenly she smelled her breakfast burning and ran to take care of it. When she came back, they were gone. She saw the cloud of dust to the south-west moving toward a rider on the hill. Apparently one of the Walking L men had gone ahead and picked up the trail.

Linda stood by the window for several minutes, letting her breakfast get cold. Somehow it didn't make sense. She couldn't quite believe Clark Hudson would stoop to horse stealing. And if he had, he wouldn't have been thoughtless enough to leave horses for the Walking L riders to use to trail him.

She ate her breakfast, but her mind was toying with an idea of checking on Jed's suspicions. The rustlers' trail had led to the south-west. The Broken Wheel was in the opposite direction. Clark Hudson couldn't be in both places at once.

Her favourite buckskin pony was still in the corral and she saddled him. It was a hot morning for late May, and she let the pony take his time. She couldn't explain the relief she felt when she came over the hill above the spring and found Clark Hudson working on a gate in the little pasture fence. She rode down to the fence and Clark stopped work, wiping the sweat from his face with his bandana.

"Good morning," he said, a wide grin on his face. "Pretty hot morning for riding around, isn't it?"

She laughed. "I'd rather ride than fix a fence. Have you been at that all morning?"

"It seems like I've been at it for a century. Not looking for a job, are you?"

She barely heard what he said. Her eyes had suddenly fallen on a horse standing in the corral by the barn, less than fifty yards from the gate Clark was building. Without checking the brand, she knew it was Blaze, Jed Porter's favourite horse.

"If you'd stayed on the job, you might be done now," she said sharply.

The grin left his face. "What do you mean by that?"

Linda pointed at the Walking L horse. "When did you bring him here?"

Clark looked, and surprise swept over his face. Linda wondered if it was caused by sight of the horse in the corral or because she had recognized it.

"I never saw that horse before," he said, and started toward the corral.

Linda reined her buckskin after him. "That happens to be one of the horses stolen from the Walking L last night," she said. "Where are the others?"

He kept walking without a word. At the corral he looked long at the horse, then turned and yelled toward the house. "Sam!"

Linda waited as a fairly small man came to the door of the house, feeling his way with a cane. A shock ran over her as she realized he was blind.

"Where have you been?" the blind man asked. "I

thought you promised me you'd tell me when you left."

"I haven't been anywhere," Clark said, and glanced at Linda.

"I heard you get your horse and ride away not half an hour ago," the blind man said.

Clark nodded. "That's when they brought us this extra horse. Sam, it looks like somebody is trying to stick us with horse stealing." He turned to Linda. "How many were taken?"

"Ten," she said, not knowing whether she was talking to a horse-thief or a victim of an attempted frame-up.

"I wasn't near the Walking L last night," Clark said. "Somebody wants to pin this rustling on me."

"Uncle Jed is mighty sure you were behind it," Linda said. "If he finds this horse here, he won't need any more proof."

Clark nodded. "Somebody had that figured. But if I'd stolen the horses, do you think I'd have brought one here? I haven't completely lost my mind. And where are the others? Somebody figured to get away with the other nine horses while your uncle was trying to hang me for stealing this one."

It made good sense. No matter what else he was, Clark Hudson was no fool. And leaving this horse in the corral would be a fool's trick. She believed him without hunting for more reasons.

"I'd better get this horse home before Uncle Jed finds it here," she said.

He grinned. "It might keep Jed from blowing his lid." He took the rope she handed him and climbed into the corral.

"Who would try to frame you?" Linda asked as Clark led the horse out of the corral.

"Probably somebody who wanted some horses and

decided to take advantage of Jed's love for me and the Broken Wheel to get away with them."

She accepted that explanation and took the rope from Clark. "I'd better be moving before Uncle Jed happens this way."

"Thanks, Miss Porter," Clark called after her. "I hope Jed catches the rustlers."

She urged the buckskin all the way back to the Walking L. If she didn't beat Jed back to the ranch, she'd have a hard time explaining where she got the horse. But luck was with her, and she turned the horse into the corral unnoticed.

It was well after noon when the crew came into the ranch yard, driving the nine horses. Jed dismounted and stamped into the house.

"We got all of them but one," he announced. "Blaze wasn't in the bunch."

"He's in the corral," Linda said, hoping her voice didn't betray her secret.

Jed walked to the window and stared out. "I'll be hanged!" he muttered. "I was sure he wasn't there this morning."

"Where did you find them?"

"West of the Broken Wheel about a mile," Jed said triumphantly. "There were a couple of gunnies with them, but they lit out when we opened up on them. I went on down to the Broken Wheel. Thought maybe I'd find Blaze there."

Linda busied herself at the table. "And if you had?"

"We'd have had a hanging right there and then. I know Hudson did that rustling or hired it done, but I can't prove it."

A rider came into the yard and Jed went to the door. Linda heard a rumble in the old man's throat like the growl of a dog, and he stamped outside, slamming the door behind him. She left her work and hurried out to the porch. The rider was Milly Hayes. She had dismounted at the hitchrail and was coming toward the house.

"That's far enough," Jed said sharply, and strode off the porch and out toward the girl.

"You're not very friendly," Milly said indignantly, stopping with one hand perched on her hip.

"I don't aim to be," Jed said testily; then his face and voice softened. "It ain't your fault, I guess. But you're just not welcome here and you never will be."

Milly frowned. "I guess I wasted a ten-mile ride out here. I thought I was doing you a favour, but apparently you don't want favours."

"People don't make a practice of doing me favours. What favour could you do me, anyway?"

"A special delivery letter came in today. I brought it out." She took a letter from her pocket and handed it to Jed.

He took it with a grunt. "Thanks," he mumbled, looking at the letter. "But what I said still goes."

"I may be back," Milly said, and went to her horse. "And I may take you off your high horse. I can tell you something else. You're biting off a hunk of trouble if you're hiring that man your letter's from. I know Hank McCabe. He's a handy man with a gun, but it will take a better man than you to control him. He didn't spend that ten years in prison because he was railroaded."

Milly wheeled her horse out of the yard.

CHAPTER VI

After Jed Porter had left the Broken Wheel without finding his other horse, Clark went back to work on the fence, finishing it before sundown. He had Linda to thank for believing his story and taking the Walking L horse with her. Otherwise, Tom Morton might not have had a ranch manager when he got to the Broken Wheel tomorrow with his herd of whiteface cattle. Porter meant business. He was only looking for an excuse to hang Clark. Linda had taken away that excuse.

Morton arrived before noon the next day with thirty head of purebred Herefords. They were exceedingly fat and sleek for this early in the season. As Clark watched them pour through the gate into the little pasture along the creek, he thought that any cattleman would be proud to own a herd like that. They were a far cry from the thin, rangy longhorns that had been running over this valley.

"They can't rough it quite as well as the longhorns," Morton said, stopping his horse beside Clark and looking proudly at the herd. "But they'll put on more pounds in a lot shorter time. Bring better prices, too."

"And they'll bring Porter down on us with guns talking, I imagine," Clark said.

Morton shrugged. "Maybe. I hope not. I want to make money here. It will be a little rough tending to the cattle and fighting off Porter. But I brought you what you'll need to handle him, I think." He motioned to the riders hazing the last of the cattle into the pasture.

"Cowpunchers or gunhands?"

"A little of both," Morton said. "Wes Surge is a good steady cowhand. He's the short one, a little on the heavy side and practically bald. But he knows cattle and he's a fine rider and roper. He can handle a gun if he has to. I don't know much about Kelly. He's the slim beanpole. I just hired him. Seems to know cattle. The redheaded youngster there is Del Knox. He's a fair hand with cattle but he's not very ambitious. I didn't hire him to punch cows. If Porter gives you any trouble, he'll be the biggest help to you."

Clark nodded. "Gunhand?"

"Claims to be. And the way he can handle a shooting iron, I don't doubt him at all."

Clark looked over the three men as they dismounted. Surge shut the gate while the other two rolled cigarettes. "How long have you had Knox?"

"About ten days. I started looking for a man like him as soon as I sent you up here. I was afraid you might need an extra gun or two."

"I'll almost bet on that. Porter is mighty ringy, especially since I started putting this fence in. We'll be lucky if we get the cattle through to fall in shape to sell them."

"The cattle will be no trouble on the river with all that grass."

"It will take a fence to keep them there, and a lot of people have wire clippers. Besides, their hides aren't tough enough to turn rifle slugs."

Morton frowned, "You really think it will come to that?"

"I don't know," Clark confessed. "If we didn't fence any more of the creek, it might not. But this pasture isn't big enough for thirty head through the hot part of the summer."

Morton's jaw pushed out. "We'll fence it all. If Porter

wants to build a lane to water and keep up the fence there, he's welcome to. But I'm not going to let all my land go idle just to please an old coot like him."

"There aren't enough posts or wire up here to fence all that."

"I anticipated that. I don't think Hayes ever finished his fence. So I bought a wagon load of posts and wire in Victor. I've got a man bringing it out now. He should be in Antelope this afternoon. Better meet him there, and on the way out here from town you can drop off the posts where you'll be needing them."

Clark nodded. "I just hope we can get the posts set before somebody makes off with them."

"That's a chance we'll have to take. The boys all know they're going to have to build a fence. Got a place for them to bunk?"

"In the house. It's a bachelor's den, so we can find a place to throw down some bedrolls."

Morton was gone and Clark had just finished showing the new men around the place when a visitor came from the direction of town. Clark went out to the hitchrack when he recognized Milly Hayes.

Milly smiled a greeting and dismounted. "That's really a fine bunch of cattle," she said.

"It won't be many years until cattle like that will take the place of longhorns. Did you bring out my mail?"

"I would have if you'd had any. I just stopped by to give you a little piece of news that might interest you."

"Something about Porter?" Clark asked suspiciously.

Milly nodded. "How did you guess?"

Clark grinned. "All the news I get lately is about Porter. And it's generally bad news for me."

Milly looked at him, a smile playing at her lips. "Do you think I'm bad news?"

"I didn't say that. You haven't told me yet what news you have."

"I took a special delivery letter out to Jed Porter yesterday. The return was Hank McCabe. Does that name mean anything to you?"

"Nothing at all."

"It will," Milly predicted. "He's a gunslick. One of the best. He's been in the pen for ten years. Porter could only have one thing to discuss with him."

Clark nodded. "Could be. Porter is pretty set on getting me out of here."

Milly swung up into her saddle. "Maybe sometime I I can bring out some good news."

Clark grinned, pushing the thought of McCabe back in his mind. "There's no law against you coming out sometime when you don't have any news."

"I might do that, too." She reined her horse around. "But I thought you ought to be on the look-out for McCabe. He's not an easy man to handle. And he isn't particular how he does a job he's hired to do."

Clark nodded. "I understand his kind. Thanks for the tip, Milly."

Milly left and Clark went back to the house where Nixon had dinner almost ready.

"What did she want this time?" Nixon asked darkly.

Clark looked at the hitchrack several yards from the house, surprised that Nixon could recognize Milly's voice from such a distance. "She just stopped to tell me Porter is hiring a gunslick."

"Watch her, Clark," Nixon said solemnly. "You can't trust her no farther than some of the new hands you got."

Clark frowned. "You don't like them, either?"

Nixon shrugged. "I didn't say I didn't like them. I just don't see a man like you do. Clothes or manners don't mean much to a man without eyes. I wasn't too happy about some of the things I saw in that young kid, Knox. He's itchy-fingered."

"That's what Morton told me," Clark said. "He hired him just for his gun. We may need it."

Nixon shrugged. "Maybe. But he'll bear watching. That itchiness isn't all in his fingers."

At dinner, Clark formed his own opinion of the men. Morton's description of them seemed accurate. Before the meal was over, he had selected Wes Surge as the man to leave in charge of things whenever he was gone. Kelly struck him as just a man with a job and Knox was a kid with a special talent that he wanted everyone to recognize. But Surge was a steady, straight-thinking man, a man Clark instantly trusted.

Leaving orders with Surge for the work of the afternoon, Clark headed for Antelope to meet the man Morton had sent up with the posts and wire. The wagon wasn't there when he got to town and he pulled up at the hitch-rack in front of Lardey's store.

The store was empty except for Milly, who was perched on a stool behind the dry goods counter leafing through a catalogue.

"Going to buy a lot of things?" Clark asked, grinning.

Milly spread her hands. "On the salary I get here? But a girl can look, can't she? What's on your mind?"

"I'm expecting to meet a man here, is there a stage or hack line here?"

Milly shook her head. "The only thing that comes into Antelope on schedule is the hot wind in the summer. Looking for someone?"

"Only the one you told me might soon be coming to the Walking L."

Milly nodded. "He'll come, all right. But he'll have to do it on his own power. There's no transportation in or out of this dump."

A horse came down the street and stopped in front of the store. Through the window Clark saw Linda Porter swing down and come up on the porch.

"Another customer," he said. "Think you can handle this rush of business?"

"Any time I can't handle her, I'll let you know about it." There was no humour in Milly's voice.

Clark glanced quickly at the little frown on Milly's face as Linda came through the door. Linda crossed to the counter and laid out a list of things she wanted.

"Has your uncle cooled down yet?" Clark asked of Linda as Milly started to fill the order.

Linda shook her head. "He's still smouldering like a volcano. He thinks you stole those horses but he can't prove it."

"Does he think I'd be dumb enough to leave them that close to my place if I stole them?"

"He isn't trying to be reasonable," Linda said, checking some of the things Milly laid on the counter. "He wants to think it was you, so he does."

"You might remind him he's got something worse than horse thieves to worry about," Milly said, setting a box of crackers on the counter.

Linda turned quickly. "What do you mean by that?"

"I mean he's over a barrel and he knows it."

Clark found himself as much in the dark as Linda seemed to be. But before he had a chance to try to figure out Milly's meaning, another rider came down the street.

Clark went out on the porch.

The rider stopping at the hitchrack was of medium build, a little on the sunny side of forty, Clark guessed. Clark had encountered cold eyes before, but never had he seen such a frigid stare as was focused on him from the pale blue eyes of this man. Before the man dismounted, Clark had him tagged. He had seen men like him in that

B.W.R.—3

fight down in Kansas. A tough hand who made his way through life hiring his gun.

The man swung down and came around the hitchrack. "Where's the town?" he demanded in a raspy voice.

"You're in the middle of it," Clark said.

The man looked around and spat contemptuously into the dust. "Some town. Who are you?"

Clark frowned. "A fellow who minds his own business."

The man's faded eyebrows pulled together. 'You don't say," he said softly. "Are you from the Walking L?"

Clark shook his head.

"Where else could you be from?"

"There are several ranches down Antelope Creek," Clark said, jerking a thumb toward the south and east. But he had the man tabbed now. When he asked about the Walking L, he might as well have shouted that he was Hank McCabe.

The man came up on the porch. "I like to get things straight, mister. What outfit do you ride for?"

"My own," Clark said. "Maybe you're thinking about starting on a job you were sent for to do. If that's the case, you'd better wait till you see Porter and get your name on his payroll."

Clark heard a gasp behind him and realized that Linda had come out of the store. But he was watching the man in front of him. His words had struck home. Even the man's stony face yielded that information.

"You're Hudson," the man said with conviction.

"That's right," Clark said, pushing away from the post where he had been leaning. "Does the name sound that bad to you?"

"Maybe." McCabe stood there, apparently undecided whether to force the issue now. There was no provocation, but men like McCabe didn't work on provocation. Money hired their guns. McCabe's decision was suddenly made for him as Linda came running across the porch.

"Stop it, you two!" She ordered. "Are you really Hank McCabe?" she demanded, turning to the gunman.

"Yeah," he said.

"Then you can just get right back on your horse and get out," she said.

McCabe's white eyebrows shot up. "Oh? Don't tell me you're Jed Porter?"

"I'm his niece," Linda said sharply. "And we don't want men like you on the Walking L."

"Well, now," McCabe said slowly, "that wasn't exactly the idea I got from Porter's letter. Think I'll ride out and see."

He turned and went to his horse, swinging into the saddle and riding down the street without a backward glance.

"I can't believe Uncle Jed would hire such a man," Linda said, watching him go.

"Looks like your uncle might be getting a little desperate," Clark said, and stepped off the porch toward his horse. Down the road he had spotted a wagon coming. He decided suddenly in favour of meeting it before it got to town.

CHAPTER VII

It was after sundown when Clark got to the Broken Wheel headquarters with the man Morton had sent with posts and wire. They had strung the posts and spools of wire along the boundary between the Broken Wheel land and the open range claimed by Jed Porter. Tomorrow the work of putting up the fence would begin.

"Itchy is gone," Nixon announced the minute Clark stepped into the house.

Clark frowned. "Knox?"

Nixon nodded. "Pulled out about an hour after you left for town. Too much work here, I reckon."

"Where did he go?"

Nixon shrugged. "I doubt if he knows himself. He thinks he's too good to work."

"He'll have to build fence tomorrow."

Before supper was ready, Knox rode in and unsaddled his horse down at the corral. Clark met him on the porch.

"Where have you been, Knox?"

Knox grinned. "Doing a little work for you. Over at the Walking L."

Suspicion rose in Clark. "What were you doing over there?"

"Visiting would be a nice word. Spying would be more accurate. There's nothing like knowing what's going on in the enemy camp to keep you one jump ahead of them."

"We don't need spies," Clark said sharply. "Anyway, I doubt if there are any secrets on the Walking L."

Knox shrugged. "I wouldn't be too sure of that. There's a mighty nice filly over there named Linda."

Clark's fist balled. "Leave her out of this."

"All right, all right," Knox said, still grinning. "I didn't know I was tramping on your toes. I found out that old man over there is just itching to get you in his gun sight."

"I don't doubt that. And he may get you in his gun sights if you go over there again."

Knox shrugged again. "I don't think so. I told them I was just a friend of one of their hands. They don't know where I work. And if they find out, they'll learn something about gun throwing if they try to push me around."

Clark frowned. Knox might be handy with a gun but he was too big for his boots. "They won't get a chance to find out about you tomorrow," he said. "We're stringing fence tomorrow."

"I didn't hire out to fix fence," Knox objected.

"Morton tells me different," Clark said. "We fix fence tomorrow."

"All right," Knox grumbled, and went on inside.

Supper over, Clark went to the corral and picked out a fresh horse. Maybe Jed Porter was just waiting to get him over a rifle sight, but he felt he had to present Morton's proposition before he started stringing wire between Walking L cattle and water.

The Walking L ranchhouse showed a light in one window when Clark rode up to the hitchrack. A dog barked down by the bunkhouse but didn't venture out. Clark dismounted and started toward the house, unconsciously hitching his gun belt around in a handier position.

The door opened only a second after he knocked, and Linda stood in the half open doorway.

"What are you doing here?" she demanded in a low tone, and he realized she had recognized him before he got to the door.

"I've got to talk to your uncle."

A frown lined her forehead. "That will mean trouble.

Can't you just tell me what you want him to know?"

"I've got to have an answer from him."

Inside, a voice boomed. "Who is it, Linda?"

Linda hesitated, her blue eyes reflecting her indecision. "Just a neighbour," she said finally.

"Better let me talk for myself," Clark said, moving into the doorway.

She gave way, worry etching her face. "Be careful," she said softly.

"I always do that." He moved past her into the big room.

Jed Porter came up out of a big chair across the room from the door as if he'd been stung. "What do you want?"

"I want to talk to you about two minutes," Clark said. "Morton brought out some more orders for me today, and I was told to make a proposition to you."

"I suppose he'd like to have me give him the Walking L," Porter snapped, his voice almost choking on his rage.

"No. He brought out posts and wire and told me to fence the rest of Broken Wheel land." Clark held up a hand as Porter surged forward to interrupt. "He said you could water at the creek if you'd keep up the lane fence to the creek."

Porter glared at Clark, his fists balled. "Bodey told me what that lying skunk said. I don't believe a word of it. You and Morton think you'll choke me out without water and pick up the Walking L for nothing. You'll find out you're wrong. I've got plenty of men who know how to use guns."

Clark nodded grimly. "So I've heard. But there's no need for fighting. All we'll gain will be the satisfaction of whittling each other to pieces. There's room for all of us here."

"That's what Hayes said. Then he tried to fence me off from water. Now you admit you're aiming to fence off the creek. Nobody's keeping Walking L off Spring Creek."

"We're making you a good proposition," Clark said. "You can water at the creek and have no trouble. But if you start cutting the fence I'm putting up, there will be trouble."

"Then get your guns oiled up," Porter shouted, "'cause we're going to start cutting as soon as we find wire between us and the creek."

Clark wheeled toward the door, barely noticing the worry on Linda's face as he strode out into the yard. He looked at the lighted bunkhouse as he mounted his horse. If McCabe or some of his kind down there were on the prowl now, he might expect a bullet in the back as he left. He wouldn't get it from the house. Porter was ready to fight, but he'd wait until his enemy was facing him, Clark guessed.

But only silence rode with Clark out of the yard. Not even the dog bothered to bark. When he reined in at the Broken Wheel corral, Knox stepped out of the shadows of the barn to meet him.

"I see you got back in one piece," Knox said.

"How did you know where I went?"

"You rode off to the southwest. The Walking L is the only place over there. I was curious to see how bad you got banged up, so I waited for you."

Clark frowned. "Well, are you satisfied?"

"Yeah," Knox said, turning toward the bunk-house. "But I didn't think you could go in there and come out without a scratch."

Clark watched him go. Knox not only wanted to spy on the Walking L; he seemed to want to spy on everybody. As he turned his horse in the corral, Clark made a mental note to watch Knox more closely.

Clark decided in favour of beginning the fence at the

far end, down close to town, leaving the creek closest to the Walking L cattle free of fence for a while. It might be that Porter would change his mind and accept Morton's proposition if given time to think it over. Surely he could see that the law was all on Morton's side.

A halt had been called for noon and the men were climbing into the wagon to head for the Broken Wheel and dinner when Clark saw Milly Hayes riding toward them from town. Clark had his horse this morning, and he reined away from the wagon.

"Go ahead," he told Surge. "I'll catch up with you."

Surge slapped the lines over the team and the wagon moved up the creek toward headquarters. Clark turned toward his visitor and waited until she reined up a few feet away.

"Bad news again?" he asked.

She nodded. "You must be a mind reader. I'm afraid you'll get to think that's the only kind of news I know."

"It seems to be the only kind of news there is," Clark said. "What's wrong this time?"

"It's not such bad news for me. But it might be for you. Fred Hayes escaped from the sheriff while he was taking him to Lincoln to the pen."

Clark frowned. "He'll be caught. And it will go harder with him when they do get him."

Milly shook her head solemnly. "Fred will never be caught. You don't know him. Remember how he threatened to get even with every one who had rail-roaded him?"

Clark, thinking back to the trail, remembered it well. But he hadn't been able then to figure out who had been on the receiving end of Hayes' threat.

"You think maybe, he'll try to get me?" Clark asked.

"It's something for you to think about," Milly said. "You were the foreman of the jury that found him guilty."

"But we didn't furnish the evidence that convicted him."

"Maybe he'll look at it that way. Maybe he won't. Fred is a pretty hard man to deal with when he gets worked up. Remember, he's got twenty years in the pen waiting for him no matter what happens. He doesn't have much to lose. My guess is he'll do some killing before they catch him, if they ever do."

"I hope not," Clark said, swinging into his saddle.

"Finding you managing his old ranch won't make him feel any friendlier toward you," Milly said.

"I'll keep an eye open for him," Clark said. "But why are you telling me? It could turn out, now that you've warned me, that I'll be able to capture him and turn him back to the law. After all, he is your cousin."

Milly nodded. "That's right. But he's a desperate man now. Whether or not he was guilty of killing Luke Porter, he'll be a killer now. I don't want my friends killed because of my loyalty to a cousin."

Clark nodded. "I appreciate what you've done, Milly. I hope Fred and I don't cross paths while he's on the loose."

"Be careful if you do," Milly said, and reined her horse around toward town.

The fence building moved along slowly. It seemed to Clark that only Surge took any interest in his work. Kelly was a passably good worker, but Knox was almost worthless on the handles of a post hole digger.

It was past the middle of the afternoon and they had put up almost half-mile of fence when Knox, who was paying attention to everything but his work, spotted a rider coming from town.

"Lots of company today," he said. "Wonder if this one is as pretty as the one who came out to chin with the boss this morning."

They had set an anchor post deep here on this knoll and had one wheel of the wagon blocked up off the ground now, using it to stretch the wires between this and another anchor post two hundred yards back.

Clark gave the wheel a final tug and Surge stapled the wire tight to the big post. Relaxing then, Clark took a look at the oncoming rider. It wasn't Milly. As the horse came closer, Clark saw that the rider was just a youngster and the horse didn't even have a saddle.

"It's that kid from down at the store," Knox said, and Clark wondered how he knew about Johnny Lardey.

Johnny reined up his old thin horse, his eyes wide with excitement. "Could you use another hand?" he asked Clark.

"You could probably do more work than some here," Clark said pointedly. "But you've got a job back at the store."

Johnny shook his head. "Not any more. I'm leaving there. The old man beat me once too often."

Clark went over to the boy's horse. "You mean you're running off?"

"I sure am," Johnny said determindly.

"Don't you think you're a little young to be making your own way?"

"I can get along," the boy said proudly.

"You'd better go back, Johnny."

"And get another beating? Not me."

"I'll go with you," Clark said. "And I'll have a talk with your dad."

"You can talk all you want to. He won't listen."

Clark considered the problem for a minute. It wasn't right for a kid Johnny's age to be running away from home. On the other hand, Cole Lardey didn't strike Clark as a fit man for any boy to have to live with. But Clark didn't figure Lardey as the bravest man in the world. It might be that some sense could be pounded into his head.

"What do you figure on doing, Johnny?" Clark asked.

"I'm looking for a job. I was hoping you could use me."

"This is a man-sized job."

"I can handle it," Johnny said confidently.

Clark considered another minute, then laid a hand on Johnny's knee. "I'll make a deal with you, Johnny. We'll go back to town together. I'll have a talk with your dad. I think I can persuade him to do things a little different. You try getting along with him again. If you can't make it and he beats you again, come out to the Broken Wheel and I'll give you a job."

Johnny thought about it seriously for a minute. "Will you promise that I won't get a beating when I get back?"

"You won't while I'm there," Clark said. "And I think I can persuade your dad to forget the beatings."

"Well," Johnny said hesitantly, "all right. But if he gives me a thrashing, I'm coming right out to the Broken Wheel and call for that job."

"It will be waiting for you," Clark said. He turned to the other men. "Finish this stretch here, then set posts till quitting time. I probably won't come back this way."

On the way to town, Clark questioned Johnny to locate the immediate cause of his decision to run away.

"I was out at the Walking L this morning," Johnny said. "A man there gave me a dollar. That's more money than I ever had in my life. Dad saw it when I showed it to Milly at noon. He tried to get it from me and I wouldn't give it to him; it was mine. Then he got his cane and beat me. He took my dollar too." Tears were in the boy's eyes.

The blood ran hot through Clark. He was going to have an understanding with Cole Lardey before he left Antelope.

The hitchrack was empty when Clark and Johnny swung down in front of the store. Lardey met them on the porch. He ignored Clark and turned burning eyes on the boy.

"Run off, will you?" he shouted. "Just wait till I get my cane."

"He's going to wait a long time for that," Clark said, stepping in front of Johnny. "You're not going to use that cane on him again."

Lardey faced Clark, the anger burning higher in his face. "Who's going to tell me how to treat my boy?"

Clark took a step forward until he was talking almost in the storekeeper's face. "I am, Lardey. You took a dollar from Johnny today that didn't belong to you. You're going to give that back to him. And you're not going to use that cane on him any more. Understand?"

Rage swept over the stooped man, choking him till his words were barely coherent. "I'll kill you!" he screamed.

Lardey swung a fist that Clark had no chance to duck. But the blow only sharpened the anger burning in Clark. His fist shot out, rocking the storekeeper back against the front of the store. He stepped forward quickly, following up his advantage.

Lardey fought furiously, driven by wild rage that destroyed what little judgement he had. But Clark's attack was cold and calculating. His fists chopped through Lardey's guard and cut slashes in his face. Lardey screamed like a wounded animal and charged away from the wall, driving Clark all the way off the porch, where he lost his footing and fell on his back.

With a triumphant yell, Lardey dived for Clark. But Clark rolled away, scrambling to his feet by the time Lardey got up. Lardey drove in, his fists better aimed now. But his blows landed only infrequently. And in between those blows, he was being shaken by heavy jolts from Clark's fists.

Blood was trickling from the storekeeper's nose and there was a streak of red at the corner of his mouth. Still he refused to quit. "I'll kill you!" he sobbed. "I'll kill you!" And he bored in again.

Clark retreated suddenly and Lardey, his swollen eyes brightening, followed. It was then that Clark drove a hard right and left into the storekeeper's face and Lardey went down.

"Now then," Clark panted, standing over Lardey. "Dig up that dollar and give it to Johnny. And promise there'll be no more beatings. If I hear of any more of that, I'll come back and finish what I started here today."

Lardey sat up, cursing through split lips. He dug a dollar out of his pocket and threw it at the boy. Then he got to his feet and staggered to the door of the store.

"You'll pay for this, Hudson. I'll get you for it."

"Just remember what I told you, Lardey. No more beatings for Johnny."

Clark got on his horse as Lardey disappeared inside the store. Giving Johnny some final words of encouragement, he rode out of town. He didn't take the trail for the Broken Wheel but cut over to the creek and dismounted. He spent half an hour there, washing his face and resting. Lardey had put up a much harder fight than he had expected.

When he did mount again and take the trail for home, the sun was getting low in the west. He was relaxed in the saddle, deep in thought, when the slanting rays of the sun struck something bright off to his left and he jerked up his head. He realized that it was a piece of metal, a gun barrel, at the corner of a jutting rock in the bluff. But before he could move, something hit him with a force that lifted him from the saddle and threw him into the deep grass. The horse bolted up the creek.

He didn't lose consciousness. He knew he'd been shot but there was no pain now to tell him where or how badly he was hit. He did wonder if the dry-gulcher wouldn't come over to see how good his aim had been, so he remained motionless and waited. But apparently the sharpshooter was satisfied with his job without checking the results.

After a few minutes, Clark tried moving. The wound was high up in his shoulder, but it was bleeding freely. He sat up, trying to fasten something around the wound to stop the bleeding. But he had to give it up. It was out of his reach.

He got to his feet, but everything began whirling around him. Before he realized it, he was flat on his face in the grass again. If he got to headquarters, he'd have to crawl. And it was still about three miles.

He realized the hopelessness of his situation; still he began moving tediously forward. He thought he might have a chance if he could only stop the bleeding. But he couldn't do that.

He wondered vaguely who had been the marksman. Probably Cole Lardey, he thought. But it really didn't matter now. Things were beginning to whirl about him even when he remained quiet. He saw his horse waiting a hundred yards ahead. If he could just get to him! But he knew now he couldn't. And the horse wouldn't go on to the ranch where his empty saddle would bring a quick investigation.

He tried to crawl farther and the effort brought on a merry-go-round of fanciful spires and bright-eyed demons. He tried to hang on to consciousness, knowing it was his only hope. But he felt it slipping away.

CHAPTER VIII

The coming of Hank McCabe to the Walking L marked a change in the life of the ranch. Before he had been there an hour, the regular hands who were at head-quarters began to show their resentment. Linda watched the change with renewed worry. Even Jed Porter seemed to be uneasy after holding a conference with the new man.

An hour after she got home from town, where she had interrupted a threatening fight between McCabe and Clark Hudson, a rider came into the ranch yard. She had never seen the man before. He swung down from his saddle and came up to the house as though he didn't have a care in the world. He was a young fellow, Linda saw as she watched him from behind the living room curtains, with flashing blue eyes, red hair, and a reckless grin.

She answered his knock, and his eyes widened with interest when he saw her. She waited for him to announce his business, but he only stared, his grin getting wider.

"Is there something I can do for you?" she asked a little irritated.

"You've done it," he said softly.

Linda frowned. "Now look, mister," she said frigidly. "What do you want?"

He winced. "You don't have to call me mister. The name is Knox. Del Knox."

"All right, Mr. Knox. What are you looking for? A job?"

Knox shook his head. "No. I happen to know one of the fellows working here on the ranch. I thought I'd drop by and see him."

Linda pointed to the bunkhouse. "You'll find him down there unless he's still out working."

Knox laughed. "He won't be working," he said positively. "Hope I see you again soon."

She didn't answer and waited only until he had turned toward the bunkhouse to shut the door. Moving quickly to the window, she watched Knox go to the bunkhouse and walk in as though he owned it.

For several minutes he didn't reappear, and when he did, the new man, McCabe, was with him. She wondered if McCabe was the friend Knox had come to see or whether he had just struck up an acquaintance with him.

They moved down to the corral and spent half an hour there, apparently talking earnestly. Jed came out of his room and went outside. He stopped and talked to the two men for a while, and when he came back to the house, the worry lines in his face were deeper than usual.

Linda forgot about the two men down by the corral as she turned her concern to her uncle who had just gone back into his room. He had been a hard working, hardheaded man ever since she had known him. It had been more than ten years now since she and her brother, Luke, had been orphaned and Jed had brought them to live with him.

But in spite of his hard-headedness, Jed had never been a worrier until Fred Hayes started fencing off Spring Creek. Even when the homesteaders had first moved into the valley, it had been Luke who had become excited and wanted to drive them out. Jed hadn't worried. He had what he wanted: control of Porter Valley and the promise of water from Spring Creek as long as he wanted it. But when the fence started going up, Jed changed overnight. Worry ate into his time and health. Stubbornness replaced the reasoning he had once shown.

The conviction of Fred Hayes had eased the tension in

the old man for a while. But Clark Hudson's appearance to manage the Broken Wheel had brought it back. And since Milly's visit yesterday, that tension had become noticeably stronger.

Linda had been at a disadvantage with Jed all the years she had been with him. For Jed Porter hated women with a hatred most men reserve for poisonous snakes. She was certain he had sent her away to school more to get her out of his sight than to satisfy any desire to give her an education. Only since the trouble had come up along Spring Creek had he made her feel that she wasn't a burden to him.

When she looked out at the corral again, Knox and McCabe were gone. Knox's horse was gone from the hitchrack, too, so he apparantly had finished his visit with the gunman and left the ranch.

Jed was restless through supper, barely touching his meal. Clark Hudson came then with his ultimatum concerning the fence to go in along Spring Creek. That did nothing to soothe the old man. But in all fairness to Clark, Linda had to admit he was giving Jed a chance. That was more than Fred Hayes had done. On the other hand, she couldn't blame Jed for distrusting Clark and Tom Morton. Hayes had promised Jed he could have all the water he wanted. He hadn't kept the promise. Would Clark Hudson?

Linda spent a restless night herself. She couldn't forget the hard set lines in Clark's face as he went past her out of the door after his quarrel with Jed. He would not be an easy man to push around.

McCabe didn't make a move to saddle his horse and ride out with the other men the next morning. Evidently his job was to stick close to headquarters, for Jed made no objections to McCabe's apparent laziness. It didn't please Linda to have McCabe around. She instinctively disliked and distrusted the man. But she made no objections to Jed.

Johnny Lardey rode his old thin pony into the yard about the middle of the forenoon. He came straight to the house, and Linda met him at the door.

"Got a note for your uncle," Johnny said.

Jed came up behind Linda. "Who's it from?" he asked.

"Milly sent it," Johnny said. "She said it was important."

Jed's face drew down into a scowl. "Milly?" He took the note and went back into his room without even thanking Johnny for his trouble.

"I've got some cookies in the kitchen," Linda said. "Want one?"

Johnny's eyes brightened, but he looked back over his shoulder toward the trail from town. "I've got to get back right away. Dad told me to hurry."

"It won't take but a minute. Come on in."

Temptation quickly overcame the boy's reluctance, and he followed Linda through the living room to the kitchen. Linda filled a little sack with cookies and gave it to him.

"Gee," he exclaimed, eyeing the cookies. "Thanks. But I'd better not take more than I can eat before I get back to town. Dad would flog me for taking them."

Linda frowned. "I don't see why. You didn't beg them. Anyway, you'll have time to eat them all before you get to town."

Grinning widely, Johnny went back to his horse. Linda watched him, and her smile turned to a frown as she saw McCabe waiting by the horse. For the first time since she had seen the man, there was a smile on his face now as he spoke to the boy.

Johnny replied hesitantly, looking the man over carefully. Linda couldn't hear what was being said, but she saw McCabe talking earnestly to the boy. He led him to the corral and, taking a rope from his saddle, showed him some clever handling of the loop.

McCabe could be a good cowhand, Linda thought as she watched him. Johnny was duly impressed and warmed to his new friend. Finally McCabe boosted Johnny on to his bony horse and fished a silver dollar out of his pocket and gave it to the boy.

The expression on Johnny's face as he left the ranch yard was assurance that Hank McCabe had made a new friend. Linda wondered about McCabe. An enemy of men; a friend of children. He was a strange man indeed.

Linda went back to her work. Jed didn't put in an appearance even when she called him for dinner. She didn't ask any questions. That was the way of being certain not to find out anything. Jed would tell her what was wrong if he wanted her to know. It must have something to do with the note Johnny had brought.

About the middle of the afternoon, Jed came out, his face drawn and haggard. He went straight to the corral without a word and got his horse. Linda watched him leave the yard, then went back to her dusting.

Her work took her into Jed's office. She had almost finished the office when, coming to Jed's desk, she found some paper wadded into a corner of a box on the desk top. She took it out, started to toss it into the pile of waste paper she had gathered, when the initials, M.H., on the paper caught her eye.

For a minute she held the paper. This was the note Johnny had delivered this morning. Those initial could belong only to Milly Hayes. Temptation was strong in her.

The office door behind her opened suddenly. She turned quickly, still clutching the paper, a wave of guilt sweeping over her although she hadn't read a word of the note. Jed stood there, the lines deep in his forehead, his eyes literally blazing.

"What's that you've got?" he demanded, pointing at the paper in her hand.

"Just a piece of paper I picked up on your desk while I was cleaning," she said quickly. "I haven't read it."

He strode forward and jerked the paper from her hand. "Why should you deny reading it? Unless you've read it and know it's something that is none of your business."

Linda backed away from the desk and started toward the door. "I don't read any of your things," she said.

He turned a fierce gaze on her. "If you breathe a word of what's in this note, I'll horsewhip you."

"I didn't read it," Linda said desperately. "I don't know what's in it."

In all the years she had been with him, she had never known him to be like this. There was a look in his eyes that frightened her, the kind of look she had always associated with a maniac.

Jed leaned against the desk and stared unblinkingly at her for a minute. "All right," he said finally. "Just be sure you keep hands off my stuff."

He turned back to his desk, and Linda was glad to escape the room. The things that Milly had said in her note apparently had driven Jed close to the breaking point.

Linda felt she had to get out of the house, to ride somewhere, anywhere, and let the wind whip some of the tension out of her. She saddled her buckskin and left the yard.

The pony headed east toward Antelope and Linda let him go.

She hadn't gone half a mile when her attention was caught by a saddled horse close to the creek bank. She looked around for the rider but she couldn't see him. Then she reined up suddenly. The horse wasn't ground-reined. That meant he had probably thrown his rider. She rode

closer to the animal before she recognized it as Clark
Hudson's horse.

She turned her eyes along the creek bank, wondering
what could have made the horse throw his rider. Then
she saw Clark, a hundred yards downstream, face down
in the grass. She nudged her horse that way, dismounting
when the animal began to shy.

One glance at Clark told Linda a big part of the story.
He had been shot and was either unconscious now or
dead. Kneeling, she quickly felt for his pulse and found it,
weak but steady.

Her first-aid training at school came to the front now
and she quickly dressed the wound, using part of his shirt
and her own neckerchief to make the bandage. She got
the bleeding partially stopped, but he would have to have
better care, and soon. She couldn't do what should be
done here in this damp grass where the night's dew would
soon settle over everything this close to the creek.

She looked at Clark's horse and realized it would be a
waste of valuable time to try to get him on his horse.
Running to her own horse, she mounted and put the
buckskin to a gallop. Minutes later, she reined up in the
yard of the Broken Wheel.

The blind man, Nixon, was the first one to come to the
door. "That you, Clark?" he called.

"It's Linda Porter," she said quickly. "Clark's been
shot. You'll have to have a wagon to bring him in."

"Sure," Nixon said. He didn't ask for any details, but
turned to the men behind him and barked out orders.
Linda was thankful for the blind man's efficiency.

Three men came out of the house, and two of them
hurriedly harnessed the team and hitched up. Knox
came over to stand by Linda's horse. She was surprised
to find him here and wondered if he were just riding the
grub line.

"I didn't expect to see you again this soon," Knox said smoothly.

"What are you doing here?" Linda asked. "Bumming a meal?"

He tried to look offended. "How can you say that? I've been earning my keep building a fence."

Linda frowned. "You mean you're working here?"

"It ain't play," Knox said, spreading his hands.

"Why aren't you helping hitch up?" she asked impatiently.

"Three of us would just get in each other's way," he said easily.

"He's too lazy to work," Nixon said sharply, feeling his way across the yard to the wagon. "Got them hitched up, boys?"

"Ready," the short pudgy man said, and helped Nixon up to the spring seat.

Linda wheeled her horse out of the yard and led the way down the river trail. The sun was gone and twilight was fading to dusk when they reached the spot where Clark still lay unconscious.

It took only minutes for the men to load the unconscious man into the back of the wagon. Linda tied her horse to the back end-gate and rode in the wagon, using a coat to pillow Clark's head. Knox was going to ride with her, but the short man, Surge, ordered him to ride Clark's horse back to the ranch.

At the ranch, two of the men carried Clark into the house and Linda followed them. She redressed the wound, checked his pulse which hadn't lost any of its strength, and turned to the men waiting.

"He'll make it, I think. But he'll have to have good care."

"I'll give him the best that a man without eyes can do," Nixon said.

"We'll see to it he gets what he needs," Surge said. "It might help a lot, though, if you could drop in once in a while and check on us."

"It would be a big help," Knox said softly.

Surge frowned. "She'll be coming to see Clark, not you," he said sharply.

"I'll come by every chance I get," Linda said. "He really ought to have a doctor look at that wound. If it starts to bleed again or shows infection, get one and call me. I've had some training." She started toward the door. "I'll have to get home now. I'll be back tomorrow."

Knox reached the door ahead of Linda. "I'll see you home, Linda. It's dark outside."

"I can get home all right," Linda said frigidly, trying to get past him.

"If anybody sees her home, I'll do it," Surge said. "But if she thinks she can get there alone, I ain't doubting her. How about it, miss?"

"I'm not afraid," Linda said, but her eyes strayed to Knox.

Surge caught her glance. "Kelly," he said, "you help Sam look after Clark. I'm riding to the Walking L with Miss Porter."

Linda smiled her thanks. She wasn't afraid of the dark. But with men like Knox and McCabe on the range, she felt safer in the company of a steady hand like Surge.

CHAPTER IX

It was a couple of days later that Tom Morton showed up at the Broken Wheel. Clark had been looking for him. He was propped up in bed, fretting away the time, when he heard the horse come into the yard shortly after noon.

"Don't recognize the way that horse walks," Nixon said as he listened.

Morton stopped in the doorway. "Anybody home?" he called.

"I wouldn't be if I could get away," Clark called back.

Morton came on into the back room. "You're a pretty sight," he said, grinning. "Haven't you learned how to dodge yet?"

"I know how but not always when." Clark shifted across the pillow at his back. "I suppose you'd ought to ask me how things are going on the ranch. But I'm going to ask you."

"I just came from the boys working on the fence," Morton said. "Wes Surge is pushing them, but he's not getting much out of Kelly and nothing out of Knox. The wire is being cut just about as fast as they can fix it up."

"He's been hard enough to keep down the way it was," Nixon said.

Clark frowned. "He never told me that." He looked at Nixon. "You knew that, didn't you, Sam? Why didn't you tell me?"

"There wasn't anything you could do about it," Nixon said. "What you didn't know wasn't hurting you."

Morton rubbed his chin thoughtfully. "I'm sorry if I spoke out of turn. I just supposed he'd been told."

"I won't be down much longer," Clark said. "We'll post guards. And when we catch the man with the clippers, we'll make him wish he'd never seen a barbwire fence."

"From what Wes tells me, you'll have to take it easy for a while. We don't have to have that big pasture right now."

"We can't expect to make much off those Herefords if we have to keep them cooped up in that little pasture all summer."

A worried frown tugged at Morton's forehead. "I know. But we won't make anything if you get up too soon and take a setback. You wait till you're on your pins again; then we'll talk about what to do."

Morton left, and Nixon frowned as he listened to the horse leaving the yard. "He sure has got a breaking out around the mouth," he mumbled.

"Don't blame him," Clark said. "Nobody told him that I didn't know. I'm glad he did tell me. I'm some manager if I don't know what's happening on the place."

"You'd have been told as soon as you were able to do anything about it."

Time dragged heavier than ever for Clark now that he knew things weren't going right outside. Linda came again in a couple of days, but this time she was all business. Clark felt the wall between them.

"You can start moving around in a day or so," she said when she finished examining the wound.

"I'll never be able to thank you for what you've done the last couple of weeks," Clark said.

"Don't try," she said, and Clark thought he detected a note of irritation in her voice. "Don't feel obligated to me. And don't hold it over my head."

Clark frowned. "I don't see how I could hold this over your head. It ought to be the other way around."

"Just because I helped you once doesn't mean it's a habit. I'd have done the same for a crippled calf."

Clark whistled softly. "Jed's raising a fuss about you coming over here, is he?"

Linda turned toward the window. "No. I've just been doing a little thinking on my own." She came back to the side of the bed. "You don't understand the situation. Uncle Jed is an old man. He's put his life into the Walking L. He's never bothered anyone who didn't bother him. Now you're trying to take all he's got away from him. That fence you're putting up will ruin him completely if it's finished."

"We're giving him a chance to water his stock at the creek by keeping up a lane fence," Clark said, knowing his argument wouldn't stand up in the face of Linda's present line of reasoning.

"This was all his when he came in here," Linda said. "I'll admit he made a mistake by settling up at the head of the valley instead of down here on the creek, but you surely don't expect me to call a man a friend who would take advantage of that mistake to rob everything from an old man."

"I'm working under orders," Clark argued weakly.

"No man who is a man will sell his self-respect for a job."

In a way Clark saw her point of view, but he thought of his own situation. He was bound on his honour to stay by Morton for at least a year to pay his debt. Linda didn't understand that and she wouldn't understand it even if he told her.

"A man can't keep his self-respect if he breaks his word," Clark said.

Contempt was in her face. "What kind of a person would promise to ruin a helpless old man?"

Clark frowned. She was talking herself into a frame of

mind that refused the admittance of reason. That came from association with Jed Porter, he guessed.

He flexed his healing shoulder. "I wouldn't say a man who can do what's been done to me and the Broken Wheel since I came here is exactly helpless."

Anger flashed in her eyes. "Are you accusing Uncle Jed of shooting you?"

"No. But you said yourself that he controlled everything around here until I moved in. I didn't shoot myself. So, according to that, it must have been somebody he controlled."

Tears glistened in her eyes. "I wish I'd never seen you."

She whirled out of the house and Clark sank back on his pillow, almost wishing the same thing. Now that Linda was gone, he realized the one thing he had been waiting for each day was her visit. There'd be no more, and if he ever crossed her path again, the friendliness that had marked her visits before today would be missing.

Nixon came in from the other room, a frown on his face. "You must have had a poor way of thanking Linda for what she's done."

Clark nodded miserably. "Seems like it. Jed Porter has her thinking his way now."

Nixon shook his head. "That's a rotten shame, I thought she had the makings of a sensible girl."

Clark hunched himself up on his pillow. "There doesn't seem to be much love lost between you and Porter."

Nixon grinned. "I think my mother named the dragons in my bedtime stories Porter."

The shoulder healed, and Clark got out of bed to move around the house, working the arm as much as he thought he dared to get his strength back. Wes Surge came in Saturday noon with news that they had completed a mile of the fence and kept that behind them repaired.

"The boys want this afternoon off," he said. "We

figure nothing will happen in daylight that close to town. So I told them it was all right. They'll have to be back to go on guard tonight. Sam says we've got to have a lot of stuff here in the house, too."

"We haven't stocked up in a long time," Nixon said. "We're low on coffee, sugar, and flour. I thought I'd ride into town with Wes, if you think you can get along all right."

Clark laughed. "You act like I was a baby. I'll bet I can ride better and shoot straighter right now than any man in the crew."

It was lonesome with everyone gone from the ranch. Clark moved around the house restlessly. Morton had been here only once since Clark had been shot. And Linda hadn't been back since the day she had made her stand and put the wall between them, a wall he could see no way around, over, or through. She was loyal to Jed Porter, a loyalty he had to admire even though he thought it was misplaced. And he would uphold the word he had given Tom Morton. The conflict between Linda and him was unavoidable. He had realized that from the start. But it did nothing to fill the hollowness in him now when he thought of not seeing Linda again.

The sound of hoofbeats took him to the window. Four riders had halted down by the corrals and were dismounting. Clark didn't recognize any of them. He wondered why they hadn't come on to the house. Suspicion tingled through his blood, and he reached for his rifle. A voice shouted from the corral, but no man was in sight now.

"Hudson, come on out."

Clark didn't answer. His suspicion had changed to conviction. Those riders were up to no good. He checked the rifle to see that it was fully loaded, and knelt beside the window.

"Hudson, we know you're there," the man yelled from the corral. "You might as well speak up."

"What do you want?" Clark yelled.

"Come out with your hands up."

"What for?"

"You're leaving this country, and we're seeing to it you get a good start."

Clark frowned as he considered this. This was Jed Porter's move, he guessed. Jed, whether or not he had ordered the shooting, knew by now that he had been shot. Apparently he was also aware that Clark was alone on the ranch this afternoon. There would be no better time to get rid of him. For without him, Surge and the rest of the Broken Wheel crew would be easy to overpower. Morton himself had told Clark that without him, he couldn't expect to hold the Broken Wheel.

Clark supposed it should be an honour to be considered so important by both friend and foe. But right now his importance was taking on a peculiar hue. If he yielded to the demands of the men down by the corral and walked out, the chances were he wouldn't get out of the valley alive.

"If you want me, you'll have to come and get me," Clark yelled.

A bullet ripped into the house. Clark waited, fingering the rifle impatiently, looking for a target. Other guns opened up and he saw that the raiders had made use of the minute or two since they dismounted. At least one man was at each corner of the barn. The other two seemed to be behind the heavy corral fence.

Waiting for his chance, Clark answered a couple of the shots, the rifle jolting back against his shoulder and bringing a stab of pain. It was spoiling his aim, too, he realized. He switched to the other side of the window and braced the rifle against his other shoulder. It was a little awkward getting a sight and squeezing the trigger, but it didn't hurt his healing shoulder to fire from this side.

His aim was better, he soon discovered, for he heard a yell down at the corral. Evidently he had tagged one of the raiders. Bullets broke out the top sash of the window and began wrecking the kitchen utensils behind him. Plaster dust filled the air and nearly choked him.

He got more bullets and kept up his fire. But he soon realized that the two men behind the corral had moved. Evidently they were circling to come up on him from another side. He watched for these flanking movements, caught one man running for the trees to his right, and cut him down. But there were still three, and at least one of them had made the safety of the trees. From there he could move in easily on the side of the house.

He ran to the side window, saw the man dodging through the trees, and took a quick shot that held the man tight behind a tree. But when he got back to the front window, he found that only one gun was speaking from the barn. Another man had taken advantage of his lapse of vigil from the front to dash for the trees. It would only be a matter of minutes until they would have him surrounded.

Struck with an idea, he suddenly ducked low and ran back into his corner bedroom. This room had only one small window. From it he saw the men dodging through the trees towards the house. It would be perhaps two or three minutes before they realized he had stopped firing. Then they would have to gather enough courage to rush the house.

Clark considered his chances. He could stay in this room and perhaps pick off one, or two if he were really lucky, as they came through the front door. But there were at least three gunmen out there. One of them would get him. But if he were outside when they came in, it might be a different tale.

He heard a shout outside. Evidently they were setting themselves for the rush. Running to the corner, Clark jerked up the trap door. It was a small hole but he thought he could squeeze through. Laying the rifle close to the edge of the hole, he lowered himself into the opening. It was a tighter squeeze than he had expected. He was half-way through when he heard running feet outside and realized the raiders were rushing the house.

Frantically he wriggled himself downward. If they caught him stuck there in this hole, he wouldn't have a chance. His hips went through and he dropped to his shoulders. Here again he had to wriggle, hands above his head, to get through.

The outside door burst open as he pulled his arms through the hole. But he ducked his head and one hand back through and grabbed the rifle. As quietly as possible, he pulled the trap door shut behind him. He heard a yell as the door dropped in place.

"He's in there. Let's get him."

Clark, kneeling in water that struck him almost at the waist, recognized that raspy voice. Hank McCabe was one of the raiders. In Clark's mind that was the final bit of proof needed. Milly had said McCabe was working for Jed Porter.

While the men above cautiously advanced on the little bedroom, Clark crept toward the edge of the house, holding the rifle above the water with one hand. There was about a two-foot space between the water and the floor of the house, but it wasn't enough to allow fast movement.

Above there was a shout and running feet, then consternation in the exclamations of the raiders as they found the room empty. Clark reached the edge of the house and was debating his next move when a gun began roaring from down the creek. Clark hurriedly waded to the edge of the spring and peered cautiously over the bank. Downstream two hundred yards was Wes Surge, using his rifle rapidly.

The men inside burst out of the house and dashed wildly toward the horses at the corral. They were carrying only six-guns, and Surge was out of their range, so they didn't even try to answer his fire. Rifle bullets dug up spurts of dust around the men as they raced for the corral.

Only three men had been in the house, but when the four horses raced away, Clark noticed that one horse was carrying a rider drooped limply over the saddle.

Surge came running toward the house. When he saw Clark, limp from weariness now that the excitement was over, staggering up to the front of the house, he let out a whoop.

"What in blazes was going on here?" he demanded.

Clark told him as nearly as he could. Then he asked, "Why are you walking?"

"Sam and me were held up just this side of town. They didn't take nothing but our team. Left us afoot with the wagon. I had my rifle in the back of the wagon. I got it and started back here. Sam and I figured something like this might be in the wind. That's a mighty long walk for a guy like me that hates walking."

"Looks like you saved my hide by doing it, though. Where's Sam?"

"I told him to stay with the wagon. I hated to leave him alone. But he couldn't walk all the way back here."

"I'll change to some dry clothes and we'll go get him," Clark said.

"I'll do it," Surge said. "You rest. You've had your daily exercise." He grinned. "Swimming with your clothes on! And at your age!"

Clark answered his grin. "I'd rather swim than get a dose of lead poisoning."

CHAPTER X

Clark was in the saddle less than a week after the raid on the Broken Wheel. His arm and side were still weak but he found that they hampered him very little. Guards had been stationed every night along the fence and the wire had been cut only a couple of times in the last week. The fence building was going forward faster now that Clark was back at the job. There was still a wide gap for Walking L cattle to get through to water. When that gap was finally sealed off, Clark expected war to erupt if it didn't before.

But he didn't expect the development that came just after noon a couple of days later. Clark was building fence with the rest of the crew when a rider on a bony horse came down the slope to the creek bottom where they were working. Clark laid down the hammer he had been using to staple the wire to the posts and turned to meet the visitor.

"Where are you headed for in such a hurry, Johnny?" Clark asked as the rider pulled up.

"I just got there," Johnny Lardey said, sliding off his barebacked mount, holding a little rifle in one hand. "I'm after that job you offered me."

Clark rubbed his chin. "You mean you're running away again?"

The boy nodded vigorously. "I sure am. Dad gave me a beating this morning. I'd warned him what I'd do if he did that. He locked me in that back room, but I bribed Milly into bringing me something to eat, and I got away when she opened the door."

The men had taken advantage of the chance to knock off work for a few minutes and had gathered around the boy. Surge put in a question now.

"Wouldn't it have been easier to have climbed out the window?"

Johnny shrugged. "It would have been if there was a window. But there's only a hole about a foot square. That room is like a prison. Anyway, I'm here and I'm ready to take that job you offered me."

"I guess it's waiting for you," Clark said. "Don't you expect your dad to look for you?"

"Sure," Johnny said. "And he'll come here, too, because I told him where I was going if I ran off."

Surge whistled softly. "That's fine!" he said in disgust.

Knox grinned. "Don't you think the four of us can handle Cole Lardey?"

"It's just more trouble," Surge said. "And we've got plenty as it is."

Johnny looked concerned. "I don't want to be any trouble. I'll work hard."

"Don't worry, Johnny," Clark said. "We'll get along."

Clark gave the boy one of the lighter jobs and soon found that he was doing more work than Knox and Kelly combined. Johnny wasn't afraid of work, that was certain.

The visit from Lardey wasn't long in coming. Milly Hayes was with him when he came over the hill and spurred his horse viciously down the slope. Johnny pressed against Clark.

"Don't let him take me back," the boy begged.

"He won't," Clark promised.

"That's for sure," Surge added softly, moving in on the other side of Johnny.

Lardey jerked his horse to a halt a few feet in front of Clark, and Milly reined up behind him.

"Get your horse and come home, Johnny," Lardey commanded, ignoring everyone but the boy.

Johnny's chin was high but his voice trembled when he replied. "I'm staying here."

"You do as I say!" Lardey screamed, and started to swing off his horse.

"Stay on your horse, Lardey," Clark said sharply. "Johnny told you he was staying here."

Lardey slid back into his saddle, wild rage twisting his face. "You keep your nose out of this, Hudson! That's my boy and I'll do as I please with him."

"You're not going to touch him. Remember what I told you before."

"I don't care what you told me," Lardey said, kicking loose from his saddle again. "I'm going to get that boy."

"If you get off that horse, I'll finish what I started down at the store the first time Johnny ran off," Clark warned, moving forward.

Lardey, half off his horse, caught himself and slowly slid back into the saddle. He scowled at Clark, breathing hard in an effort to hold back his rage. "I'll kill you some day, Hudson!"

Knox, leaning against the wagon to one side of the group, spoke up. "Don't you think you're running off a little too much at the mouth, Lardey?"

Lardey turned his scowl on Knox. "I ain't saying half as much as I'm going to do," he threatened, then turned back to Clark. "I'll have the law out here, and we'll see who keeps the boy."

"I'll abide by the law," Clark said. "But remember, if you call in an official of the law, he might find out a lot of things besides whose boy this is."

The angry red drained out of Lardey's face for a moment, then poured back heavier than ever. "I'm going to get Johnny back," he yelled.

Milly Hayes, who had been sitting silently by, spoke to Lardey now. "Why don't you shut up, Cole? You know you're better off without the boy. And he's a lot better off without you."

Lardey wheeled on the girl. "Johnny ain't your boy," he shouted.

"If he was, I'd let him stay where he wanted to," Milly said. "I'm going back."

She wheeled her horse. Lardey stared belligerently at the men facing him. "I'll get Johnny back!" he yelled, and wheeled his horse to follow Milly.

"I wouldn't blame anybody for running off from that sidewinder," Surge said as he turned back to his hammer.

"I'm scared of him," Johnny said, staring after the riders. "He was awful mad."

"He'll get glad again," Clark said. "Let's go to work."

The fence building proceeded at a good pace with Johnny doing his share. When they got to headquarters after work that afternoon, Clark took Johnny into the house where Nixon was working. In spite of Nixon's uncanny memory and ability to handle himself, there were several jobs around the kitchen that he couldn't do alone.

"How would you like to have a helper around the house, Sam?" Clark asked.

"If you mean Johnny, nothing would suit me better," Nixon said.

"How did you know Johnny was here?" Clark asked.

"Well, since you told me you promised Johnny a job, I've been looking for him every day. Lardey isn't a man to stop beating a kid. That's his calibre. I knew Johnny was here just now because I heard him walking in the other room."

Clark turned to the boy. "Suit you, Johnny?"

"You bet," Johnny said. "Sam and me got along fine while he was at the store."

It was the next morning that Wes Surge discovered the whiteface bull dead at the far end of the little pasture. Clark rode with him to look at the animal. It took no more than a glance to tell that the bull had been shot.

"Porter?" Surge suggested.

Clark nodded. "I don't know who else would gain anything by killing this bull. Not Lardey. He'd do anything to get at me. But the whole country knows these cattle belong to Tom Morton."

"What are you going to do about it?" Surge asked as he and Clark walked back to the fence.

"I think I'll ride over and have a talk with Jed Porter. An animal like that will cost two hundred dollars to replace."

Surge nodded. "Looks like you might have some use for Knox after all. This is what Morton hired him for."

"I'll go alone this time," Clark said. "No good starting a shooting war till we have to. With Knox along, I'd be asking for it."

Clark didn't have to go to the Walking L house to find Jed Porter. The old man was down at the corral with most of his crew looking over a dozen or more wild young horses that apparently had just been brought in from the range.

"What do you want, Hudson?" Porter demanded belligerently as Clark reined up.

Clark leaned an elbow on the saddle horn. "I thought you might know something about the man who shot my herd bull last night."

Porter's eyes flashed angrily. "I suppose you think I did it?"

"Who else would profit by killing him?"

Porter pushed away from the men around him. "I don't know who did it, Hudson," he said, "but when you find out, I wish you'd tell me. I'd like to reward him."

Clark frowned. "I doubt if you'd have half the trouble I would in finding the man."

Porter's face reddened. "Now listen here, Hudson," he snapped. "You're not going to pin that on me. I'm glad somebody did it. But it wasn't me. If that's all you want here, you'd better hit the trail."

"Want me to give him a boost?" McCabe said at Porter's elbow.

"Just what were you doing last night, McCabe?" Clark asked suspiciously.

McCabe moved out from Porter. "Think maybe I shot the bull?" he asked quietly.

Clark nodded. "Could be. You seem to be the gunslick in this crew."

"Well, I didn't," McCabe said. "But if you want to play like I did and make something of it, it's all right with me."

Clark realized he was getting into deep water. While he might beat McCabe in a man to man gun-fight, he couldn't handle the entire Walking L crew.

"I'm looking for the man who shot that bull," Clark said evenly. "Throwing guns isn't going to find him. When I get him located, it might be different."

"Showing yellow," McCabe said scathingly.

Clark eyed the gunman. "Not a bit, McCabe. If you're the man who shot the bull, I'm calling your hand. Draw or drag. If you're not, then I've got no quarrel with you."

McCabe hestitated. He wanted this fight; it showed in his eyes. It was what he had been hired to do, Clark guessed. But he didn't want to admit killing the prize bull. To a man like McCabe, killing a man was an honour, but killing a helpless animal was the work of a coward.

While McCabe hesitated, Porter stepped in. "Get back, McCabe," he said. "This is between me and Hudson."

He turned to Clark. "Now then, if you've had your say, get off the place and don't come back."

"I've had my say," Clark said. "Except this : if I catch anybody shooting my cattle, I'll plug him just like I would any lobo."

"If you get any more killed, don't come back here accusing us unless you've got proof. Next time it won't be so healthy for you."

"You might keep your gun-happy boys off the Broken Wheel, too," Clark said hotly. "They've been there twice. If they come again, there'll be some dead ones to bring back."

He wheeled his horse and kicked him into a gallop. He couldn't blame Porter too much for getting his ire up if he wasn't guilty of killing the bull. But the incident certainly hadn't improved relations between the Walking L and the Broken Wheel. He thought of Milly's prediction that there would be blood on the grass in Porter Valley before there was peace. That prediction seemed to be coming closer to reality all the time.

He rode into his corral, head down in thought. The silence didn't alarm him; the rest of the crew should be out working on the fence now. He dismounted at the corner of the barn, still without any premonition of danger. Only when he felt a gun pressed into his back did he snap his thoughts back to his surroundings.

"Turn around easy, Hudson," a voice said. "I want to talk to you, not kill you."

Clark turned slowly, and his surprise was complete when he recognized Fred Hayes behind the rifle. Hayes was standing back in the doorway of the barn out of sight of the house.

"Come back here in the barn," Hayes ordered.

Clark obeyed, thinking of the warning Milly had given him. "What do you want?"

"Not what you think," Hayes said as if reading his mind. "Maybe I ought to kill you for handing down that verdict against me. But it wasn't you that convicted me." He looked out the door. "I want some grub. I was going to the house to get it when I saw you coming. You'll get it for me."

"You're dodging the law," Clark said. "Why should I help you?"

"Mainly because I'll have this rifle in your back," Hayes said. "I was framed for that murder. I aim to settle the score before they catch me."

Clark thought of the empty cartridge he had found by the bluff close to the spot where Luke Porter had been killed. His doubts of Hayes' guilt had risen then.

"What kind of a rifle did you have before you were arrested?" he asked.

"The same kind nearly every rancher has," Hayes said. "A .44. What difference does that make?"

"I was just wondering about it," Clark said.

Hayes jabbed the rifle into Clark's back. "Forget the wondering. We're going up to the house and get a sack full of grub."

Clark moved toward the house with Hayes directly behind him. "Are you figuring on clearing your name?"

"I ain't worrying about that," Hayes said. "I'm going to get the ones that framed me."

Hayes took the bulk of the food in the kitchen while Johnny and Nixon sat motionless in the corner of the room. His sack full of food, Hayes backed to the door. There he stopped.

"Come here, kid," he said to Johnny. "You're going with me till we get to the top of the hill, just to make sure nobody gets ideas about turning me over to the law."

Johnny, frightened but game, went out of the door with Hayes. Clark could do nothing but watch as Hayes got his horse and walked to the top of the hill. There he released Johnny, mounted, and disappeared over the rise.

Clark thought of the plight of the escaped convict. As Milly had said, Fred Hayes was a desperate man now, regardless of whether or not he had killed Luke Porter. And Clark's doubt as to that was growing every day. Hayes' answer as to the kind of rifle he had owned was too sincere to be doubted. And that hadn't been a .44 cartridge he had found out by the bluff.

CHAPTER XI

The wire was cut in three places that night. Clark was out with Wes Surge fixing the fence before the sun was an hour high. Both Surge and Knox had been on guard last night. But the fence was stretched over too many miles now to be kept under close guard. Surge had seen one rider during the night, but hadn't been close enough to him to identify him or to take a warning shot at him.

Clark and Surge were splicing the wires at the second break when a half-dozen men rode over the hill and came down toward them. One look at them and Clark laid down his tools. These men were heavily armed and rode as if they were on a serious mission.

As they came closer a premonition of trouble swept over Clark. At the head of the group rode Cole Lardey. The men reined up thirty feet from Clark and Surge, guns trained on the pair. Lardey acted as spokesman.

"I'm arresting you, Hudson, for the murder of Jed Porter," he announced.

For a second Clark was too stunned to move. He looked from one man in the group to another. He saw Hank McCabe there and a couple of other Walking L riders he had seen yesterday with McCabe. The other men he had never seen before. And there was a deputy sheriff's badge on the front of Cole Lardey's shirt.

"When was Porter killed?" he asked finally.

"Last night," Lardey said. "Right down the creek a piece close to that first break in your fence. I don't need to give you the details. I came out this morning and got the body."

Clark frowned. "There wasn't anything there this morning when we fixed that fence."

Lardey waved a hand impatiently, looking around to make sure that guns were still trained on Clark. "He was back in the bluffs. But there's no question in anybody's mind that you did it."

"Clark wasn't even out here last night," Surge put in angrily.

Lardey looked at Surge as he might at a fly buzzing in a spider web. "I've got a dozen witnesses who say Jed and Hudson quarrelled violently yesterday. And Hudson threatened to kill Porter if he came on the Broken Wheel again. Jed's niece, Linda, found a note in his room asking him to come to these bluffs at sundown yesterday to discuss some business. That note, as we found by comparing handwriting, was written by Hudson."

"That's a lie!" Clark snapped. "I didn't write any note. And you don't have any of my writing to compare it with, anyway."

Lardey grinned triumphantly. "Have you forgotten the grocery lists you wrote out to bring to town? I've got a couple of them."

An idea suddenly hit Clark. "Maybe you're a good forger, Lardey."

A scowl wiped the grin off Lardey's face. "You can't lie out of it, Hudson. As for me being a forger, that's impossible. I can't write so you can read it. You killed Porter and you'll hang for murder. Get his gun, boys."

Clark had been watching for a chance to make a break ever since Lardey began producing proof of his guilt. But he had no chance. Another frame-up, he thought savagely, like the one that had convicted Fred Hayes. But he knew he had missed his shot in calling Lardey the forger of that note. Maybe Lardey knew who did it; maybe not. But remembering his grocery receipts, Clark realized that Lardey couldn't write a legible hand. Certainly he couldn't imitate another's writing.

His gun was taken and he was ordered on his horse. Surge made a move to interfere, but Clark checked him and sent him to the ranch to tell the others. There was nothing Clark could do now but wait for developments and hope he got a break.

Before he got to town he began to get a thread to work on. He had thought before that the war was aimed at the Broken Wheel. Now he wondered if it wasn't aimed at Jed Porter and the Walking L. The Broken Wheel and its ramrod, the natural enemies of the Walking L, were perfect scapegoats.

At Antelope, Clark was marched through the store and shoved into a back room and the door locked. This was the room Johnny had told about being shut in, Clark guessed.

He gave the room a quick examination by the dim light that came in through a tiny window close to the ceiling. That window wasn't more than a foot square but it did allow a little light. This room must have been built for a jail, Clark decided.

Time dragged slowly.

Sometime late in the afternoon, the silence out in the store was broken. Clark crouched against the door, and his interest quickened when he recognized Wes Surge's voice.

"I just want to talk to Clark for a minute."

"Nobody sees the prisoner," Lardey said. "Hudson is a murderer and I'm going to guard him mighty close."

"You're a liar," Surge snapped. "Clark wasn't anywhere near the place where you say Porter was killed. I've got a right to talk to him. You can come along if you want to."

Lardey laughed. "And have you gang up on me? I'd

be apt to fall for the trap! You're not going in to see him."

"Can I talk to him?" another voice asked.

Clark's interest stepped up another notch as he recognized Sam Nixon's voice.

"Want to take him a gun, I suppose," Lardey sneered.

"I just want to talk to him," Nixon insisted.

"Frisk him," Surge said. "Make sure he doesn't have a gun. Any jail in the country lets its prisoners have company."

For a moment there was silence, and Clark guessed that Lardey was considering his next move. "I wouldn't trust either one of you as far as I could throw a bull by the tail," Lardey said finally.

"We're not asking you to trust us," Nixon said. "Search me and take every weapon I've got. I just want to talk to Clark."

"All right," Lardey said after another pause. "Take off your boots, too. You're not going to slip him a knife or gun that way."

For another minute there was silence. Clark heard Nixon's boots hit the floor.

"Now I'm barefooted," Nixon said disgustedly. "Do you want me to take off the rest of my clothes?"

"Naw," Lardey said. "There ain't no guns or knives on you now, I know. Come on back here."

Clark heard the thumping of Nixon's cane as he came toward the back room. He moved away from the door and waited until Lardey unlocked it. Lardey stood there, gun in hand, while Nixon felt his way inside. Then the door went shut and the lock clicked.

"Glad to see you, Sam," Clark said. "This is a pretty lonesome place."

"I imagine it is," Nixon said, jerking a thumb in the direction of the door.

Outside, Surge spoke up. "Afraid you might miss a word or two, Lardey?"

Footsteps shuffled outside the door. "I was just making sure they weren't talking about plans for him to escape."

"Do you think he can escape from your jail?"

Lardey moved back a few steps. "He can't escape from there except through the door, and nobody goes through that door unless I say so."

Surge kept Lardey talking, but Clark's attention had suddenly switched back to Nixon. He was twisting the top of his cane, and Clark realized that the handle was coming off. Nixon motioned for Clark to come closer. While Surge and Lardey continued to talk outside, Nixon whispered to Clark.

"There's a knife inside this cane. Get it out."

The top of the cane came off, and Clark saw a small, thin-bladed knife there. He lifted it out, and Nixon began screwing the top of the cane back in place.

"Not very big," Nixon whispered. "But they'll respect it as much as they would be a butcher knife. You've got to get out of here. You're framed like a picture. If they don't figure out a way to kill you first, you'll be convicted by the court."

"I'll make it now," Clark said, fingering the knife. "I want to have a look around the place where Porter was killed. I may come to the Broken Wheel for something if I have to."

"We'll be on the lookout. If there is a saddle on the corral fence close to the barn, it's safe to come in. If there isn't a saddle there, that means the place is being watched."

"Fine," Clark said. "I'll be careful."

The voices outside stopped, and Nixon held up a finger, then pointed it toward the door.

"I'll tell the boys to lay off the fence then until Morton

comes," Nixon said loudly. "We'll do what we can to prove you're innocent." He began tapping his cane toward the door.

The lock turned and Lardey opened the door a way, his gun in his hand again. "Through gabbing?" he asked.

"I reckon," Nixon said. "You sure make it hard to find out what we're supposed to do out on the ranch until he gets out."

Lardey laughed. "He ain't getting out. Murderers hang in this state."

"Not a peep," he said softly.

CHAPTER XII

The sun came up on Clark huddled under an over-hanging bluff out of sight from the prairie above and only visible to a small section of the creek below.

He had stopped here last night close to the spot where Lardey had said Porter had been killed. Now, with light for his search, Clark began a careful examination of the entire area.

A ravine ran back into the prairie fifty yards behind the bluffs. After climbing up to search the prairie in all directions for signs of a posse, Clark dropped down into this ravine. He didn't have long to look to find the spot where the grass had been trampled and he guessed this was the spot where Porter had fallen and men had come to pick him up.

Running his eyes over the area for a likely spot for a drygulcher, he settled on one not far from the place where he had spent the night. It was only about thirty yards from the spot where Porter had fallen. But, remembering that Porter was supposed to have been killed at sundown or later, he knew a marksman would have to be fairly close to be able to hit his target.

Going back to the bluff, he searched the ground carefully. He wondered if the killer would be careless enough to kick the empty cartridge out of his rifle. Even while he was thinking about it, he had his answer. Not one but two empty cylinders were in the grass under the bluff. Apparently the first shot hadn't been perfect.

Picking up the cartridges, he examined them quickly.

The thrill of discovery ran through him. These were just like the one he had found close to the spot where Luke Porter had been killed. The same gun and probably the same killer. And it wasn't Fred Hayes unless he had another rifle cached away somewhere. For the rifle he had the other day was a .44. These shells were bigger than a .44, and his guess that they were fired from a Spencer .56 rim fire rifle was becoming a conviction.

Clark wondered how it happened that the men who had been riding guard that night hadn't heard the shooting. A Spencer .56 was a noisy thing. It had been Wes Surge and Del Knox on the fence that night. Surge had the other end of the line and Knox had been down here. Come to think of it, he hadn't seen Knox since that night. Maybe the red-head could tell him something. Anyway, he wanted to get to the Broken Wheel and check with the cartridge he had there to make sure these were the same.

He went back to the creek after taking another look over the prairie. Apparently there were no posses out this side of town looking for him yet. Nevertheless, he stayed close to the bluff on his way up the creek to the Broken Wheel headquarters.

From the protection of a chalk rock ridge jutting out from the bluff below the little pasture, Clark surveyed the ranch buildings. It was the most natural place for Lardey to set a trap to catch him. Smoke curled lazily from the chimney of the house, but there was no saddle on the corral fence close to the barn. Clark settled down to wait.

After a while, a rider came in from the south. It was Surge, and Clark kept a close vigil on him. He dismounted and went in the house, then came back to the barn and unsaddled his horse. Looking in every direction, he finally threw the saddle over the corral fence by the barn and turned his horse into the corral.

Clark grinned. The way was clear now. Apparently Surge had been out scouting around to make sure. Or possibly they had just learned that he had gotten out of Lardey's prison.

Moving down along the fence, Clark hurried toward the house. Any time now a posse could be expected to start combing this region, and the Broken Wheel would not be overlooked.

Nixon apparently heard him coming, for he had the door open when he reached the house.

"Get in here and keep out of sight," Nixon said. "You sure upset a beehive in town, Wes says."

"I figured they might have this place blocked off," Clark said.

"They will have. You'd better get some grub and a horse and hit for the sandhills. You can give them the dodge there."

"I want to get something here first," Clark said. "I looked over the spot where Porter was killed. Found a couple of empty cartridges. They're just like the one I found where Luke Porter was killed. Must mean something. If I could only find the rifle that shot these bullets! Is Knox around?"

"He came in yesterday morning for a while, then rode out again, and we haven't seen hide nor hair of him since. Think he's got something to do with it?"

Clark got the other empty cartridge from the cupboard. "He was riding fence along the line where Porter was killed. He should have heard the shots. I wanted to ask him."

The cartridges were the same. Clark looked at the dent on the rim of the shell made by the firing pin. "Fired from the same gun," he said musingly.

Surge came into the house. "You'd better hit the trail," he said. "It won't take them long to be all over this country."

Linda was still too stunned by her uncle's murder to be aware of much that went on in preparation for the funeral.

After the funeral, Jed's lawyer asked her if he might not read the will then and save her the trip to Victor or him the trip back to Antelope. At first it seemed like a sacrilegious thing to do so close in the wake of the funeral. But to her stunned mind, nothing really mattered a great deal, and she gave her consent.

Sitting in Lardey's store while the lawyer opened the will and read it, she got the jolt needed to bring her back to the realization that life must go on. The lawyer's voice was solemn and unruffled, but the words struck Linda like coals of fire.

"And to my beloved niece, Linda Porter, I give and bequeath all of my earthly possessions."

There was more, but Linda barely heard it. She didn't know what she had expected; she really hadn't thought about it. But now she realized the responsibility that had been thrown on her.

When she left the store, her mind was whirling. It occurred to her that she might sell the Walking L and get out from under all the trouble. But it had been home to her. And it had been Jed's very life. Now he had left it to her, and she would carry on with it.

A frown tugged at her face as she rode up to the house. McCabe was sprawled in a chair on the porch, his feet on the railing, and beside him on the steps was Del Knox. She was afraid of Hank McCabe and she was sure he knew it. As for Knox, she had a loathing of him and his lazy, insolent ways. He had been on the Walking L more than he had at the Broken Wheel where he was supposed to be working. And he let it be known that she was the attraction that held him here.

"I brought you some company to cheer you up," McCabe said, grinning as she dismounted. "Del ain't got a thing to do but make you happy."

"I don't need cheering up," Linda snapped. "Hank, take this horse to the corral and unsaddle him."

McCabe took his feet off the railing of the porch. "Well, now," he said slowly, "when did you get the job of giving orders here?"

"Today," Linda said sharply. "Uncle Jed left me this ranch and everything on it."

Knox grinned. "I'm on it, so I guess that leaves me to you, too."

"If you belonged to me, Mr. Knox," Linda said spunkily, "the first thing I'd do would be take a black-snake and whip that grin off your face."

McCabe laughed, but Knox's face reddened. "Now look here," he said, and his voice held an unpleasant edge, "I don't take that kind of talk from nobody." He got up off the steps of the porch.

Linda was half-way up the walk to the porch when he started coming toward her. She thought of running; her horse was just behind her. But her pride and anger ruled against that. She had no gun, but her quirt dangled from her wrist.

She kept her steady pace forward and started to brush past Knox as if he were just a dog in the way. With a muttered curse, he grabbed her arm and wheeled her around.

"You don't need to act so high and mighty," he said. "You'll come down to our level now that Jed's out of the way."

Anger and fear mingled in her to give her a strength

she didn't know she had. She wrenched free of his grasp and brought the quirt around in a whistling blow. It caught Knox across the shoulder and wrapped around his neck, cutting in to the blood.

With a yell, Knox reeled backward, lost his balance, and fell. Linda hurried up the steps of the porch. McCabe hadn't moved, but he was laughing, looking at Knox. She stopped just short of the door into the house.

"Hank, put away my horse," she ordered.

McCabe got up, the laughter still in his eyes. "Yes, ma'am," he said in mock respect. "That quirt talks mighty loud." He went down the steps and stopped to laugh again at Knox, just getting to his feet.

Linda went on into the house. She couldn't remember ever before seeing McCabe break that stony mask that had always been on his face. Evidently life looked rosy to him. But he was dangerous. She knew that. Tomorrow she would fire him and she'd find some way to get Knox off the place.

She went into her room and locked the door. She didn't want any supper and she resolved not to go outside her room again tonight. She checked the pearl-handled .38 Jed had given her several years ago. Loading it, she put it under her pillow. She could kill a man if she had to, she thought.

She was long in going to sleep, her mind whirling with the problems that faced her. But after weariness finally took command, she didn't waken until the first rays of the sun were slanting through the window. She got her breakfast and went out to begin her first day of operation of the Walking L. Her initial job would be to fire Hank McCabe and boot Del Knox off the ranch.

She stopped in amazement on the porch. Three saddled horses were at the hitchrack. One of them was her own. McCabe was loitering on the porch again.

"What are you doing here?" she demanded.

"Waiting for the boss," he said easily. There was no laughter on his face this morning.

"You have no boss," Linda retorted sharply. "You're fired. Come on in and draw your pay."

"Don't be too hasty," McCabe said, not moving. "Del and I have a trip to make this morning, and we thought you might like to go along."

"I don't," she said, fear crawling along her spine. "Now get out of here. I'll call the men from the bunkhouse if you don't."

Still McCabe didn't move. "Won't do any good," he said. "They were looking for something to do this morning, and since you were so slow coming out, I suggested we all ride out and check the cattle. You see, nobody took care of that yesterday. So they went."

"And you stayed," Linda said, despair washing over her.

"Well, I had this other trip to make. They didn't need me anyway." McCabe got up. "Come on. We're wasting time."

"I'm not going anyhere," Linda said, starting to retreat toward the house.

Only then did she realize why McCabe had kept talking so pointlessly. His stalling had given Knox time to come through the house behind her. Now he caught her arms as she backed up.

"You won't quirt me this time," he said, his fingers biting savagely into her arms. "Come on, Hank. Let's ride before some of the boys decide to come back to see what happened to us."

Linda fought furiously, scoring a minor triumph when she stamped the heel of her foot on Knox's foot. He yelled in pain but held on, and McCabe came to his aid. Within two minutes she was tied on her own horse.

"Where are you taking me?" she demanded.

"You'll get there just as well without worrying your head about it," McCabe said.

Linda's gun had been taken from her and her hands tied to the saddle horn. She looked around desperately for help as they rode out of the yard. But the ranch was quiet. Evidently McCabe had got rid of the entire crew. It was a clear morning and she could see all the way down the valley to Antelope. It was this view that had prompted Jed to build here rather than close to the creek.

Down the valley a couple of miles, she saw a rider, but she had no way of signalling him. To the left a little were the trees around the Broken Wheel. She thought of Clark Hudson. Yesterday she had hated him for killing Jed Porter. But now she would welcome the sight even of the man she thought was Jed's killer.

They rode over the knoll to the south-west and the valley dropped out of sight. After an hour of easy riding, they reached Rus Abbott's old soddy. Here the men dismounted and untied Linda.

"Now you've found out where we were going just as well as if we'd told you," McCabe said. "Del, put the horses around back."

"Why not the barn?" Knox asked.

"It's between us and the valley," McCabe explained. "If anybody trails us, they'll come by the barn. We don't want our horses shot up."

Knox grinned. "You're smart, Hank."

McCabe grunted. "Not so smart. Some people I know are just dumb."

Linda was tied to an old chair inside the two-room house. She glanced around, wondering where Fred Hayes was. The house showed obvious signs of being lived in. The stove was free of dust, as was the table, and there was a pile of buffalo chips in front of the stove. But neither

McCabe nor Knox seemed to notice it, or perhaps they knew Hayes had made this his hideout.

In less than thirty minutes two riders came from the north-east. McCabe's caution relaxed when they came in sight. Linda caught her breath in astonishment when they dismounted and came within the range of her limited vision. They were Cole Lardey and Milly Hayes.

Knox took their horses around behind the house, and Lardey and Milly came in with McCabe.

"Everything went off as planned, I see," Lardey said, rubbing his hands in satisfaction.

"Didn't expect anything else, did you?" McCabe said.

"Some things haven't done so well lately," Lardey said darkly. "Hudson, for instance."

McCabe snorted. "I told you what you should have done with him, and you were too dumb to see it."

Lardey frowned. "All right," he said irritably. "So I made a mistake that once. We'll get him, don't worry. Right now we've got another job." He turned to Linda. "No use beating around the bush. You can make things very easy for yourself by selling us the Walking L."

"This is hardly the way to make me feel like selling," Linda said angrily. "Why didn't you ask me yesterday?"

"Yes, why didn't you, Cole?" Milly said disgustedly. "I've been bossing this thing pretty well till you decided yesterday you'd take over. This is your idea, and I can see where it's going to get all our necks in a noose if we're not careful."

Just then Del Knox came in from tying the horses behind the house. "What took you so long?" she railed at him.

Knox shrugged. "What's the hurry? We're not going anywhere. Anyway, from the sound of things you had plenty of men to yell at without me."

"We need every man we've got in Antelope," Milly

said, pacing the floor again. "Del, you go bring them out. And get a little fire•in you."

"All right," Knox said irritably. "I'll get them. But remember, horses can't fly."

Knox went out and a minute later was riding his horse up the long slope to the east. The soddy quieted down as Milly dropped on a chair and sank into deep thought. McCabe rolled a cigarette and propped himself against the door jamb as though he hadn't a care in the world. Only Lardey seemed restless, moving around the room, smoking continuously.

The pounding of hoofbeats brought tension to the little soddy. Lardey ran to the door, almost falling over McCabe, who hadn't moved.

"It's Bixby," Lardey said, breath whistling out of him. "Wonder what's wrong?"

"Where did he come from?" McCabe asked, getting to his feet.

"We left him about a mile back on the trail to watch for trouble," Milly said.

"Looks like he might have found what he was looking for," McCabe murmured.

Bixby, a short, heavy rider, slid his horse to a halt in front of the house. "Three riders coming," he said, leaning over the saddle. "Looks like Hudson is one of them."

McCabe whistled softly. "Trouble is right."

"That's good," Milly said thoughtfully, pounding her fist into her hand again. "Get your horse behind the house out of sight, Bixby. Cole, get that box of dynamite you've had stored here ready to blast the Walking L."

Lardey moved toward the back. "I hope it's still here. I put that dynamite here two weeks ago, and somebody's been cooking and eating here."

"Nobody would run off with a box of dynamite," Milly said. "Hurry."

Lardey went into the back room, and Linda heard boards being prized off the floor. Then he came back with a small box marked explosives.

Bixby came in the front door.

"Now what?" he asked.

"It's our chance to finish this thing in one sweep," Milly said. "We've got to get rid of Clark Hudson. If that's him coming out there, he'll use the barn for a shield to get close enough to see what's up. That's a sure bet."

"So?" Cole asked, interest showing on his face.

"Anybody feel like shooting it out with him?"

McCabe shrugged. "I might. But I figure you've got a better idea."

"I have," Milly said. "A charge of dynamite at the corner of the barn would be easy and safe. And sure."

Lardey grinned. "It sure would. Come on, Hank. Let's set it."

Lardey took two sticks of dynamite and a long roll of fuse from the box and headed for the barn, McCabe following.

"Do you think he'll really walk into that?" Bixby asked.

"I'll bet anything he will," Milly said. "Bring a couple of horses back around here. He'll come nearer falling for it if things don't look too suspicious."

"How are you going to set that dynamite off at the right time?"

"That's Cole's job," Milly said. "He's an old hand with that stuff. He can time a fuse almost to the second. And he can figure how long it will take Hudson to get to the barn after he sights him. You worry too much, Bixby."

"I was on that raid with McCabe," Bixby said. "I saw that hombre shoot. I don't want any part of a scrap with him."

McCabe came back to the house in a few minutes. "It's all set," he said. "Cole's sure of himself now. He knows what he's doing with that stuff." He pointed to the top of the hill, half a mile away. "There they are. Cole's going to wait till Hudson gets the barn between him and the house and make a run for it; then he'll light the fuse and get back here."

By leaning forward in her chair as far as her bonds would allow, Linda could see out of the window. Both hope and despair struck at her. That was Clark Hudson sitting that horse out there. She was sure of it. But she couldn't be sure who was with him. If only she could think of some way to warn them. But there was no way, and she knew it.

She saw the riders moving over to get the barn between them and the house. In a minute now Clark Hudson would come down that slope. She knew it would be Clark. He was not the kind of man to let another take the risk. Milly Hayes had planned on that when she laid the trap. Soon the trap would be sprung.

CHAPTER XIII

Linda's heart was in her throat as she saw one rider move out from the others up on the slope and start down toward the barn. She saw a white flag waving from the barrel of the rifle. But dynamite would pay no heed to a flag of truce. And neither would Cole Lardey or Milly Hayes.

The rider didn't stay directly behind the barn as expected but came toward the house with regard for the shelter of the outbuilding. Linda was watching the barn closer than the rider to see when Lardey would break for the house. That would mean that the dynamite fuse had been lit. The angle the rider was taking would bring him right to the corner of the barn.

Linda, scarcely breathing, suddenly concentrated on the rider. He wasn't big enough to be Clark Hudson. He was just a small fellow, no bigger than a boy. With a gasp, she realized that it was a boy. Johnny! But would Lardey recognize him in time?

McCabe, standing motionless by the window, suddenly came alive. He whipped a glance at the barn, then stared again at the rider.

"That's Johnny," he breathed. He ran to the door. "Hey, Cole," he shouted. "That's the kid!"

At that moment Cole Lardey dashed from the barn door and came towards the house in a crouching run. McCabe met him just in front of the house.

"Put out that fuse," McCabe yelled.

Lardey tried to push past him. "Get back in the house, you fool. Do you want to get shot?"

"That's not Hudson," McCabe shouted, pointing. "That's Johnny!"

Lardey wheeled and stared. "The little fool!" he ejaculated.

"You've got to stop that dynamite from exploding," McCabe yelled.

Lardey pushed the gunman back through the door. "Too late now. He should have stayed where he belonged."

"How long a fuse is on that?" McCabe demanded.

"About a minute," Lardey said proudly. "He'll hit it exactly right."

"You've got time to stop it," McCabe yelled, pushing Lardey back toward the door.

"I'm not going back there," Lardey said, bracing himself. "I'd be blown to bits."

"But that's Johnny," McCabe shouted frantically, with more emotion than Linda had ever imagined existed in the man.

"So what?" Lardey said heartlessly. "He asked for it."

McCabe suddenly whipped out his gun and jammed it into Lardey's side. "Get out there and stop that blast," he ordered.

Lardey turned pale and the fear of death was in his eyes. "I can't, Hank," he whimpered. "It's too late. I didn't know it was Johnny, honest."

"What's it to you, Hank?" Bixby said. "It's just a kid."

McCabe turned scathing eyes on Bixby. "Johnny's my son," he said, breathing hard. He wheeled back to Lardey. "Get out there or I'll kill you!"

Lardey took a step, then stopped, trembling from head to foot. "I won't go. I won't die that way."

For a split second it seemed that McCabe surely would squeeze the trigger. Linda closed her eyes, nerves tense, waiting for the shot. But none came. She opened her eyes again to see McCabe dashing through the door, gun still waving in his hand. Lardey staggered weakly back against the wall.

Linda watched McCabe, afraid to look, and finding it impossible not to. He was running wildly down the path toward the barn. Johnny was just a few yards on the other side now. The gunman fired a shot over Johnny's head.

"Go back, Johnny!" McCabe screamed. "Go back!"

Johnny stopped but he didn't turn. McCabe ran on, firing another shot over the boy's head.

"Go back!" he screamed wildly.

McCabe was even with the barn when Johnny wheeled his horse and dug in his heels. The gunman whirled and started toward the house on a run. But he didn't get three steps until the whole prairie seemed to erupt out there. A wall of dirt shot through with splinters from the boards that supported the barn roof rose into the air.

Linda closed her eyes as a blast of air rocked through the little sod house. For what seemed an eternity to her, she heard dirt and pieces of boards falling. Then there was a deathly quiet. She looked out through the window again. A cloud of dust obscured everything.

When the dust began to clear she saw Johnny still riding back up the slope where the other two riders were coming to meet him. But she didn't see McCabe. And she knew she would never see him again. He had been too close to that blast.

"You fool!" Milly's voice broke the silence in the sod house. "You blundering fool!"

Lardey scowled as he came away from the wall. "Don't call me a fool, Milly. That was your idea."

"The idea was all right. But the way you handled it! Why can't you do anything right?"

"What was wrong with what I did? I set that blast so it would catch the rider. And it would have if Hank had had any sense."

"What good would it have done to kill Johnny?"

Lardey crossed the floor angrily. "I didn't know it was Johnny."

"You had time to stop that fuse when Hank first told you."

"What for? What difference did it make what happened to Johnny?"

Milly waved an arm toward the door. "Look out there and see if you can see what difference it makes to us. We've still got Hudson to fight. And we haven't got Hank to help us now."

"The crazy fool!" Lardey raved. "It served him right. We can hold off Hudson till Del gets here with the boys. Nothing to worry about."

Milly peered at Lardey through narrowed eyes. "As long as Clark Hudson is on the loose, there's something to worry about. If you'd stopped that blast, we could have held our parley with Johnny and laid a perfect trap for Hudson and whoever is out there with him. Then we'd have had easy pickings. Now we've got a fight on our hands and we're short-handed, thanks to you and your bungling!"

Lardey strode across the floor angrily. "Why didn't you run out there and pinch off that fuse if you thought of so many advantages?" he demanded.

Milly didn't answer but focused her attention on the three horsemen bunched out there on the hillside. Bixby chose the lull to ask a question.

"What did McCabe mean by saying Johnny was his son?"

"Just what he said," Milly replied. "Hank and Cole used to be partners. Hank was caught and sent up and Cole wasn't. That was the only difference between them. Hank's wife was dead, so he turned Johnny over to Cole to take care of while he was in prison. Hank didn't have the money or a place to keep Johnny when he got out, so he left him with Cole."

Linda understood now why McCabe had made up to Johnny so quickly that day on the Walking L. And she understood other things about the man that had puzzled her before.

Along with the others in the little soddy, Linda turned her attention to the men out on the slope. They had dismounted now, and each had tied his horse to the thick base of a sagebrush. Then they had dropped to the ground where the sagebrush furnished perfect cover for them.

"They're sneaking in behind that pile of dirt that was the barn," Bixby said. "They'll be pretty close."

"Nothing we can do about it till they start shooting," Lardey said. "Can't see anything stirring out there in that brush."

"Keep your guns ready," Milly ordered. "If you do see some of them, let him have it. You'll have a better chance now than you will once they get in behind that old barn."

A watchful silence settled over the house. Suddenly it was broken by a shot from Bixby's rifle. Immediately an answer came from the rubble of the barn.

"They're in there already," Milly exclaimed. "Lay low and don't give them a second's rest. Del will be bringing the rest of the boys soon."

"They'd better hurry," Lardey said as a bullet whistled through the open window. "Say, that was a little rifle. Must be a .22 musket. He can't shoot far with that."

"Don't have to," Bixby muttered. "There's only forty yards between us."

Lardey laid his big rifle across the window sill and squeezed the trigger. The roar filled the room.

"Use your hip gun," Milly shouted. "They're not a mile away."

Time dragged on, punctuated regularly, it seemed to Linda, by shots from the old barn, all of them aimed high. Occasionally a heavy rifle spoke out there, and it seemed those bullets were sometimes far over the top of the house.

"That's Sam Nixon on that big rifle out there," Milly said suddenly. "He's been shooting clear above the house. Anybody with eyes wouldn't miss that far."

"All the shots have been high," Lardey said musingly.

"I know," Milly said. "They don't want to hit Linda." She frowned. "What's Hudson doing out there? That little pop gun must be Johnny. If Nixon is handling the big gun, what's Hudson doing?"

She bent low and crossed the room to the back window. Lardey nodded after her. "You've probably guessed it."

Linda's heart sank. Clark would have to come in under fire. And the chances were he wouldn't make it.

A quarter of an hour dragged by before Milly spoke softly from the back window. "Here he comes, sneaking in like a coyote."

"Pick him off," Lardey said.

"Can't do it," Milly said. "He's watching this window like a hawk. If I shove a rifle barrel out there, we'll have a two-sided battle going. And you can be sure that kid out front will lower his aim if Hudson starts shooting. I've got a better idea."

"What now?" Lardey growled. "Something else that will backfire?"

"Not if you've got sense enough to handle your end right. We need that blind man and kid. I can use them to make Linda sign over the Walking L. We'll never get them while Hudson is on the loose."

"Let me over there," Lardey said, starting across the floor on his hands and knees. "I'll get him."

"Get back there," Milly ordered. "Let the kid and the old man think Hudson hasn't made it yet. They'll be easy to pick up then. We'll wait till Hudson makes a break for this window, then jam a gun down his throat."

Lardey came on across the floor in spite of Milly's order. "I'll do that jamming, and I hope he tries to shoot."

"Don't shoot unless you have to," Milly said. "That's an order. You've bungled things proper so far. I'm running things this time."

Linda heard Clark's footsteps an instant before Lardey leaped in front of the window, his gun pointing through.

"All right, Hudson. Drop it. Or try to use it if you feel lucky."

"He's not that dumb," Milly said from the other side of the window. She had a gun trained through the window, too.

"All right," Clark's voice came to Linda after a pause. "You've got the drop on me. Now what?"

"Climb through the window easy," Milly said. "That's what you came here to do, wasn't it?"

Clark climbed through. "It was. But I was expecting the guns to be pointing the other way."

Hands held high, Clark allowed himself to be searched for hidden guns. Then Lardey spoke to Milly.

"We could finish him off now and they'd never know out there what was happening."

"We've got him now," Milly said in satisfaction. "We might find some use for him, too. Tie him up and do a good job of it. Then put him and the girl in the other room."

Clark looked at Linda. "Are you all right, Linda?"

"They haven't hurt me yet," Linda said, twisting uneasily in her chair.

Milly laughed. "Yet is a nice word. Hurry it up, Cole."

Lardey finished binding Clark and dragged him into the other room. Then he pulled the chair with Linda still tied to it through the doorway and shoved it against the

far wall. Back in the partition doorway, he stopped.
"Now what?" he asked.

"You take Bixby's place with that gun. We'll keep
those two busy out there. Bixby, you go through this back
window and slip around and get the drop on Johnny and
that blind man and bring them in. We need them."

"Why not wait till the boys come?" Lardey said.

"We don't need the boys for this job," Milly replied.

"I wonder what's keeping them," Lardey said thoughtfully, and spun around to face the prisoners. "Hudson,
what do you know about Knox?"

Clark stared unblinkingly at Lardey. "I know he's as
dead as McCabe is," he said.

Milly stared over Lardey's shoulder. "I don't believe
it," she snapped. "Where did you see him dead?"

"About a couple of miles east of here," Clark said.

Milly frowned, then spun around. "Go ahead, Bixby.
Bring in those two. You shouldn't have any trouble with
them. But don't kill them. I want them alive."

Bixby went through the back window, and the spasmodic shooting continued. Linda spoke softly to Clark.

"How did you find out what happened?"

"One of your men saw you being taken off. He told
us, then went to round up your crew. They'll be along
later."

"Just Johnny and Sam Nixon out there?"

Clark nodded. "We're in a tough spot till your boys
get here. And that may be pretty late in the day. I sure
walked into their trap."

Clark sank into frowning thoughtlessness and Linda
turned her attention to the other room. The shooting continued regularly and harmlessly. It was almost a half-hour
before it stopped. And a minute later, Bixby herded
Johnny and Nixon through the door, giving Nixon a
vicious shove when he stumbled.

"Tie them up and put them with the others," Milly ordered. She frowned at Clark. "If you're not lying about Del, our plans might have to be changed."

"Go look for yourself," Clark advised.

"I think we will. Bixby," she said to the burly gunman, "ride over Del's trail and see if he is dead."

CHAPTER XIV

Clark shifted his back against the sod wall and looked at his fellow prisoners.

"It's my fault we're all tied up like calves at branding time," he said, disgusted with himself. "I should have waited till I was sure before charging in."

Clark leaned back to rest, and his eyes fell on the rifle propped against the far wall in the other room. He nodded toward it.

"That looks like a Spencer .56. That must be the gun that killed Jed and Luke Porter."

"That belongs to Cole," Johnny said softly.

"I sort of had that figured," Clark said. "But I couldn't find it the other night."

"Does that mean that Cole Lardey killed my brother and uncle?" Linda asked.

"It means that his rifle killed them," Clark said grimly. "It might have been Lardey himself, or Bixby, or McCabe, or even Knox who did the job."

"Or Milly," Nixon put in.

"She would hardly do the murdering," Clark objected.

"I wouldn't put it past her," Nixon said.

"What do you know about Milly?" Clark asked. "You've had her tagged as a vicious sidewinder ever since you came to the Broken Wheel."

"She is, too, Clark," Linda put in. "I saw her real nature this morning. I'm more afraid of her than I am any of the men."

"You've got a good reason to be," Nixon said. He

nodded toward the other room. "What are they doing out there?"

Clark craned his neck to see. "They're outside the door right now. Killing time till Bixby gets back, I reckon."

"I've got something to tell you that maybe I should have told before. But I thought it was my own problem. Now we're all in it."

"Go ahead," Clark said. "I'm listening."

"I'd better start at the beginning so you'll understand," Nixon said. "When I was a young sprout, I was a wild one. I had quite a bit of money, although nothing to brag about. I was raised on a ranch but I went to work in a bank.

"There was a girl there that I was crazy about. But a young rancher won her from me. That was all right. He did it fair and square. That young buck was Jed Porter."

Clark heard Linda catch her breath. "That was why you were so familiar with Porter," he said.

Nixon nodded. "I knew him well then. I got to know him better than I wanted to. Porter didn't have much money, and Hazel, the girl he married, wouldn't put up with poverty. They quarrelled, and finally she ran away from Jed. She came to me. I'd had a windfall from a relative a while before that and I had a lot of money. She threw herself at me and, being a wild young fool, I caught her and thought I had the world by the tail with a downhill pull.

"What I thought was happiness didn't last long. Porter was wild when he found out what Hazel had done. He came after me. I wasn't such a big fellow, but I was a good man for my size. I tried to avoid Porter because he was out to kill me. I knew I couldn't handle him in a gun fight. I managed to meet him in town one day when he didn't have his gun. The fight we had was something that little town probably never has forgotten.

"Neither one of us won that fight. We were more dead than alive when we quit. But Jed had hit my head a lot and somehow it affected my eyes. Within a couple of days I was blind."

Linda gasped. "No wonder you hated Uncle Jed."

"Nobody ever heard me say I hated Jed Porter," Nixon said. "If I'd had a lick of brains I wouldn't have touched Hazel with a ten-foot pole after the way she treated Jed. Well, as soon as I went blind I began to find out what Hazel was really like. My income stopped, of course, for it's pretty hard for a blind man to get or hold a job. She was mean to me, mean as Satan. She went through the money I had and pulled out."

Nixon paused, and Clark reminded him of the thing he started to explain. "What does all this have to do with Milly?"

"I'm coming to that," Nixon said. "I lost track of Hazel after she left me. Then I found she had married a man named Hayes. Does that answer your question?"

Clark nodded. "Milly is Hazel's daughter."

"And with the same mean streak running through her. I knew it before I was around her an hour. She can be just as nice-appearing as Hazel was, and she's just as full of Satan. From the sound of her voice and the way she was described to me, I'd say she looks like her mother, too."

"Maybe that was why Uncle Jed hated her so," Linda breathed.

Footsteps crossed the floor of the other room, and Milly stopped in the doorway. "What are you doing in here?"

"Killing time," Clark said. "We've already tried the ropes. We can't get them untied."

Milly nodded. "I know. Cole's an expert at that." She turned and went back to Lardey at the outside door.

"Why did you come back here where you knew she

was?" Clark asked. "I'd have thought you would have wanted to stay as far away from Hazel or any of her kin as you could."

"When you've had to live inside your own mind for thirty years as I have, you put a different value on things. I see more by feel and hearing than most men do with their eyes. I've learned to consider my blindness almost as a blessing. I don't have to wait for a man to show his colours to know what he is. The sound and feel of him when I'm around him tells me. I knew from what I'd heard that Milly was like her mother. And I didn't want any man to suffer like I did because of a woman like Hazel.

"I learned that Milly was out here and I knew about what she was here for. It was just like her mother to think she ought to have everything Jed Porter ever made, regardless of how she had treated him. She'd pass that on to her daughter. So I figured Milly was here to get Jed's ranch. I tried to be careful when I got here, but they got the jump on me one time."

Nixon paused again as if listening.

"Somebody coming?" Clark asked.

"Hard to say," Nixon said. "I thought I heard something but it was pretty faint."

Johnny had been leaning forward, listening attentively to Nixon's story. "Do you mean the day you were robbed?"

Nixon nodded. "That was the time. I had a letter I wouldn't have let Milly get her hands on for the world. I was afraid to leave it in my room. They tore up my room one day while I was out. Evidently Milly knew I had it. I rather expected that. My big mistake was in not destroying the letter. I'd always had the hope of using it some day in dickering with Jed Porter."

"Was it something against Uncle Jed?" Linda asked,

the fingers of her hands, which were bound together in her lap, twining and untwining.

"Yes," Nixon said. "It was a letter Jed wrote to Hazel just a while after she left him. He couldn't give her up, it seems, and he tried to get some money so she would come back to him. He held up a bank and killed a man in doing it. He got the money, all right, and made his getaway, but he was fool enough to write to Hazel and tell her what he'd done and that he had all the money she'd want if she'd come back to him. He didn't know then that Hazel had come to me. He thought she had gone back home.

"She got the letter all right. But I stole it from her things, thinking I might use it against Jed Porter some day, for I knew Jed would come after me when he found out that I'd taken Hazel. I carried that letter with me all the time. I should have destroyed it. That day in Antelope, Knox and Milly robbed me and they got the letter."

"So that was what Milly was holding over Uncle Jed," Linda said softly. "He was like a wild man after Milly's last visit to the ranch."

"That letter could have sent him to the gallows," Nixon said. He cocked his head suddenly and listened closely.

Milly and Lardey came back, but it was not them he had heard.

Then suddenly Fred Hayes leaped through the door, his gun in his hand, his face twisted with hate.

CHAPTER XV

"Turn around easy," Hayes snarled. "And keep your hands clear."

Milly spun around. "Fred!" she exclaimed, and there was both fear and relief in her voice.

"Easy, I said," Hayes said threateningly.

"I heard you had escaped," Milly said, friendliness dripping from her voice. "But I hadn't seen you. I was beginning to think it was just a rumour. I'm so glad you're free."

Hayes laughed. "I'll bet you are! And so is Cole."

"Yes—yes, of course I am," Lardey said hastily but with a complete lack of enthusiasm.

"Shut up," Milly snapped. "Whenever you run things, you run them into the ground. We need you with us, Fred. The same agreement we had before."

Hayes sneered. "With the same results, I suppose. A double-cross."

"You weren't double-crossed," Milly insisted. "We were standing by you. You'd have gotten your share when you got free again. Now you won't have to wait."

"You're right, I won't have to wait. I said I'd get the ones who railroaded me. I figure on doing just that."

Lardey licked dry lips. If there had ever been any courage in the man, it was gone now. But it wasn't so with Milly. She kept her brave front, stalling Hayes with a quick tongue.

"You can't very well kill a dead man, Fred. Jed Porter is dead."

Hayes' eyes narrowed. "But the ones who double-crossed me aren't dead yet."

Milly's face became serious. "Now listen, Fred. Revenge isn't going to get you anything. But you can gain a lot by sticking with us. Before this day is done, we'll clean up the whole valley."

"What good would that do me?" Hayes sneered. "I'm wanted for murder, remember? The law would come and get me and leave you with the fat again. Not for me, dear cousin."

"Who said you'd have to stay here? There are enough cattle on the Walking L and the Broken Wheel to set you up for life. We'll make a quick sale, and you can take your share from that and disappear. Can you think of anything better than that?"

Hayes nodded. "I reckon I can. Getting even for that double-cross."

Hayes raised his gun and gripped it a little tighter. The colour and courage fled from Lardey's face. His knees began to buckle.

"Don't shoot!" he screamed. "It wasn't my idea. It was Milly's."

Clark, trying to watch everything in the other room, had seen Milly's hand slip into the neck of her riding blouse. He guessed what she was after. Now, as Fred Hayes whirled back to her at Lardey's outburst, she jerked out a tiny derringer.

She fired point-blank at Fred Hayes. His answering shot rocked the room but nothing else. The tiny bullet had found its mark before he could squeeze the trigger. Hayes stumbled forward, and Milly stepped calmly aside to make room for him to fall. Then she turned the little gun on Lardey.

"I ought to kill you next. Your job was to hold his attention."

"But he was going to shoot me," Lardey whimpered.

"Too bad he didn't," Milly said heartlessly. "You only needed to keep him busy for another second. I wasn't ready. It was just luck I got him."

"In another second I'd have been dead," Lardey said, heaving a sigh as Milly slipped the gun back in its hiding place.

"Get him out of here, Cole," she said.

Lardey stooped and picked up Hayes' feet and dragged him through the door. When he came back, he glanced impatiently at the prisoners.

"Let's get this over with, Milly. We lost a lot of time with Fred."

Milly went to the window and looked out. "Bixby's coming." She turned, her eyes bright. "We'll find out about Del now; then we'll get busy."

"What now?" Nixon whispered to Clark.

"I don't know," Clark said. "She'll try to make Linda sign over the Walking L. Then it will be the end of the trail for all of us, I guess."

Bixby stamped into the house. "It's just like Hudson said," he reported. "Del's deader than a doornail."

"Well," Milly said, her eyes narrowing to slits as she turned toward the back room, "let's get to work."

She strode purposefully into the little room with Lardey and Bixby behind her. She looked over the prisoners with a penetrating scrutiny. Then she concentrated on Linda.

"All right, I'm giving you a decent chance to sign over that ranch. But I'm not going to play around all day with you. How about it?"

"I told you before," Linda said stoutly.

Milly shrugged. "All right. Have it your own way. I told you what you could expect. We'll start nice and easy." She moved closer and slapped Linda a stinging blow that left a row of red marks outlining Milly's fingers.

Clark clenched his fists behind his back, his rage mounting. Sitting against the wall, he hunched his legs up under him as if to get out of Milly's way as she stepped back from Linda.

"That help any?" Milly demanded.

Linda clenched her teeth and shook her head. "No."

Milly moved in for a harder blow. But it didn't land. Clark's feet shot out and caught Milly on the knee, throwing her back against the far wall.

Milly leaned against the wall for a moment, wild rage flashing in her eyes. "So you want to play rough?" She charged away from the wall, aiming a kick at Clark's face. He twisted and caught the boot on his shoulder.

"Come on, Milly," Bixby said impatiently. "You ain't getting nothing done that way."

Milly backed off, scowling at Clark. Clark glanced at Bixby and saw the disgust on his face. Bixby was a gunman, ready and willing to fight anywhere any time. But in a gunman's book, this was a coward's fight. And Bixby obviously had little respect for a coward.

"Get out if you don't like what's happening," Milly said.

"I think I will," Bixby said. "And you'd better not be too long getting out of here yourselves."

Bixby went out.

Milly looked over the prisoners another minute, then held out a hand to Lardey. "Give me your knife, Cole."

Lardey dug a jack-knife out of his pocket and handed it to Milly. She opened it, ran a finger lightly over the blade, then moved up to Nixon.

"You fiend!" Linda cried.

"If you don't want to see me butcher him, bit by bit, you know what you can do about it," Milly retorted.

"Don't give in to her," Nixon said.

"But she'll kill you," Linda said, a sob in her voice.

"I'd rather die than see Milly get that ranch."

Milly hit Nixon a sharp slap across the face. Nixon grinned and said nothing.

"Why don't you whittle up Hudson?" Lardey suggested.

"I might let my feelings get the best of me and cut too deep," Milly said, scowling at Clark. "I want this to last long enough for Linda to get some sense."

Lardey stared at Clark, breathing hard. 'He beat me up once. I said I'd get even."

"You'd better do it right now," Clark said grimly. "If I ever get free, you'll never get another chance."

Lardey moved in and hit Clark a blow on the mouth that brought the blood and made the room rock before Clark's eyes. He struck again, and Clark rolled back against the wall. Lardey, his eyes wild with delight, charged in again. Clark straightened just as he had against Milly. But this time he caught Lardey high in the pit of the stomach. Lardey gasped a curse as he crashed against the far wall. He slid down in a groaning heap. Milly took one look at him, then wheeled toward Clark with the knife.

"I ought to cut your heart out," she said. "But he had that coming."

She turned back to Nixon. "Get ready to watch the blood flow," she said to Linda, and dropped the knife against Nixon's arm. The blind man flinched but said nothing.

Lardey was regaining his breath. He staggered to his feet and reeled across the room toward Clark.

"I'll kill you with my bare hands," he sobbed, his voice choking with rage.

"I'll sign the papers," Linda cried.

"Don't do it," Clark said sharply.

"I've got to," Linda sobbed. "I won't let you all be butchered because of a ranch."

"That's more like it," Milly said, crossing to Linda, cutting in front of Lardey.

"Get out of my way," Lardey shouted thickly. "I'm going to kill him."

"Oh, shut up," Milly said irritably, pushing Lardey back against the wall again. "Get that paper you brought. It's all ready for her signature."

Lardey swore softly, then dug into his pocket and brought out a paper. He handed it, with a pencil, to Milly. "I'll get him yet," he said.

"As soon as we get this signature you can do as you please," Milly said.

Linda took the pencil when Milly untied her hand, but she didn't write.

"I won't sign it unless you promise you'll not harm those three," she said.

Milly frowned, looked at Lardey, then nodded agreement. "All right. All we want is that ranch. We don't care what happens to anybody or anything else. Here. Sign it."

Linda worked her cramped fingers for a moment, then signed the paper. Milly took the paper and pencil and heaved a sigh. "That does it," she said in satisfaction.

"Now can I kill him?" Lardey demanded.

Clark was sure his time had come and prepared to put up the best battle possible under the circumstances. But Milly rubbed her chin thoughtfully.

"We've got a lot of work to do, Cole. Let's get going."

"And leave this outfit here to get loose?"

"Who said anything about letting them get loose? We're taking Linda with us. We can make the Walking L crew kick in without a scrap if we've got her as hostage."

"What about Hudson and the blind man and Johnny?"

"Fires don't leave much trace," Milly said. "Come on. You bring the girl. There's some kerosene in here."

Lardey grinned. "That suits me a lot better. Beating him to death would be too easy. A fire is nice." He turned suddenly and went into the other room. "I want to be sure the fire doesn't go out before it gets to them."

He came back into the little room carrying the box of dynamite from which he had taken a couple of sticks to blow up the barn this morning.

"Hurry up, Cole," Milly said from the other room, where she was pouring a can of kerosene over the floor.

"I'll be right there," Lardey said, placing the box four feet in front of Clark. He grinned at the prisoners. "When this dynamite gets about so hot, it will explode. You can have some fun guessing how close the fire will have to get to set it off."

"Hurry up," Milly shouted.

Lardey untied Linda from the chair, picked her up bodily and carried her through the partition door. Cursing, Lardey got through the outside door with his prisoner.

Milly came back into the back room and looked at the ropes holding each of the prisoners.

"I think they'll hold till the fire burns through them. By then it won't make any difference." She glanced at the box of dynamite. "Six sticks. That should make a nice explosion."

She went back into the other room. There in the doorway she struck a match and tossed it on the kerosene-soaked floor. She waited a minute as the flames leaped high in the room and smoke curled into the little room

Then, with a hard laugh, she went through the door. where the three prisoners were.

CHAPTER XVI

Clark's eyes flashed to the floor. He had forgotten about Milly's knife. But there it was now on the other side of Nixon, half-way across the room.

He started to roll that way, but Johnny spoke excitedly. "Maybe I can kick it to you."

Clark watched Johnny strain as he edged out from the wall. With a jerk, he shoved the knife several feet toward Clark. Clark rolled then, hitching himself around until he felt the knife under him.

A hot blast of air swept in from the other room and Clark shot a glance at the partition door. The fire was almost there. Frantically, he hitched himself around until his fingers hit the knife. It cut into his flesh, but he worked the blade through his fingers until he had a grip on the handle and the blade was up in the vicinity of the ropes holding his hands.

"Roll over, Clark, where I can see," Johnny said. "I'll tell you what you're doing."

Clark rolled, and Johnny directed his movements. The tongues of flame were licking ever closer to the box, reaching out for it like greedy fingers.

"You're almost through," Johnny said breathlessly. "Hurry, Clark."

Clark put all the strength in his cramped fingers against the knife. He felt the rope give and he threw his muscles into a pry. For an instant the ropes held and Clark thought he would have to waste more precious seconds sawing again. Then they broke, and he jerked his hands around in front of him.

With two swift slashes, he cut the ropes on his ankles. Then in a matter of seconds he had cut both Johnny and Nixon loose.

"Get out of the window," he yelled.

"How about the dynamite?" Nixon said.

"It's too hot to handle now," Clark shouted. "It will explode any second. Come on."

He helped Nixon through the window, almost threw Johnny out after him, then dived through himself. He scrambled to his feet, then paused momentarily as he heard a groan.

"Must be Hayes," Nixon said close to Clark's ear.

"I'll get him," Clark yelled, spotting Hayes close to the corner of the house. "Get out of here, you and Johnny. This whole thing will go sky-high any second."

Running to Hayes, Clark grabbed him by the arms and hurried after Johnny and Nixon. Hayes groaned again but made no effort to help himself.

Clark was several yards from the house when it seemed the whole world exploded. A blast of air knocked him to the ground and he stayed there, his face in the grass.

Chunks of dirt and sticks fell around him and he waited until it was quiet before he moved. He looked first for Johnny and Nixon and saw them several yards ahead of him, lying flat in the grass.

"Are you all right?" Clark shouted.

"Sure," Nixon said. "How about you?"

"Still in one piece," Clark said.

Clark looked back at the spot where the house had stood. The charge of dynamite hadn't left enough to tell what it had been. Through the smoke and haze hanging over the spot, Clark caught a glimpse of three riders nearly to the top of the slope to the north-east. He flattened himself in the grass again and called to the two ahead of him:

"Stay down for a while. Milly and Lardey are still in sight. Let them think we went up with that blast."

"Right," Nixon shouted back.

Clark watched the three horsemen as the smoke cleared away from the explosion. They had been watching, and now they turned and went on up the slope. Hayes stirred beside Clark, but Clark made no move until the riders disappeared over the hill.

"Any water around here?" he asked then, getting to his feet.

"Some in my canteen," Johnny volunteered. "The horses are still out there."

Clark looked up on the slope toward their horses. Then behind him another horse nickered. "That must be Hayes' horse," he said, turning. "Maybe he's got a canteen."

"I'll see." Johnny ran up the gully where a bay horse, frightened by the blast, had jerked loose from the sage-brush where he had been tied and was nervously backing off, his reins trailing.

Johnny moved up to the horse carefully and caught the reins. Then he led him down to Clark.

"There's a canteen all right," Johnny said. "And there's a bedroll, a rifle, and it looks like a sack of grub."

Clark nodded. "Hayes had to be prepared to keep going if his trail got hot. Hand me the canteen."

With Hayes still groaning semi-consciously, Clark washed the bullet wound and, with a sleeve of Hayes' shirt, bandaged it the best he could. It was deep in the shoulder, close to a lung. Absolute rest was the only thing that could heal that wound.

As Clark finished with the bandage, Hayes opened his eyes and stared blankly at those around him. Finally recognition came into his face.

"How did I get here?" he mumbled. "Where's Milly?"

"She left you for dead," Clark said.

Hayes peeled his lips back in a weak attempt to snarl. "She shot me. She didn't want me around if she couldn't use me."

"You'd better not get yourself worked up," Clark suggested. "You're not in very good shape."

"I'm on the last lap, I know that," Hayes said, his voice getting clearer and stronger. "But I'm not dead yet. I've got one more job to do." He tried to sit up, but Clark held him down.

"You'd better take it easy, Hayes. That hole isn't too far from a lung. If you move around much, you might tear a hole in your lung."

Hayes sat up in spite of Clark. "What if I do?"

"You won't last long."

Hayes made an effort to get to his feet. "So what?"

"You don't want to die, do you?" Johnny asked incredulously.

"What have I got to live for?" There were beads of sweat on Hayes' forehead, but his eyes were bright now and the strength was flowing through him. "Answer me," he said, staring at Clark. "What have I got to live for?"

Clark wondered himself. "Not too much, I guess," he said finally.

"Not a thing," Hayes said, "but a long stretch in the pen. I'd rather take it this way."

"There's nothing you can do," Clark said.

Hayes laughed, a mere gurgle in his throat. "I can do plenty if I can hold on long enough." He looked down at the bandage over his wound. "You've got it tied up. It ought to hold me together for a while. I've got one job to do before I cash in my chips. Bring my horse here."

"You can't sit a saddle," Clark argued.

"Tie me on my horse, then," Hayes said through set teeth. "I've got one more job to do and I've got to ride to do it."

Clark nodded grimly.

"Bring his horse here, Johnny," he said. "I'll help him get on." After they had sent Hayes on his way, Clark hurried up the slope to the horses as fast as Nixon could travel. Johnny ran ahead and had the horses untied.

"Can't depend on Hayes to get to Milly," Nixon said. "It's up to us. And we've got to do it before they get possession of the Walking L, or we'll never see Linda alive again."

Clark helped Nixon mount. "You think if we get rid of Milly it will break up their outfit?"

"It would have before today," Nixon said. "Now Lardey realizes he's in so deep he can never get out. He'll have to be handled, too, I reckon. We'd better hurry."

Clark needed no urging.

When they came to the top of the hill that overlooked Porter Valley, he drew rein and scanned the slope. There, between the Broken Wheel and the Walking L, riding hard, were a dozen horsemen.

"That's the Walking L," Johnny said excitedly, pointing.

"I reckon," Clark agreed. "And right down here close to the ranch is somebody else." He concentrated on the rider pulling out of the Walking L yard and coming toward them. "That's Tom Morton," he said. "Come on."

Clark led the way down the slope. Morton reined up and waited when he recognized them.

"Where's the girl?" Morton demanded when Clark rode up. "I was talking to a Walking L rider a while ago. He said the Porter girl had been kidnapped and you'd gone after her."

Clark nodded. "We went after her. But we didn't get her."

"Nearly got blown to kingdom come," Nixon said. "Haven't you seen Milly Hayes and Lardey?"

Morton shook his head. "No. What have they got to do with it?"

"They've got Linda," Clark explained. "They forced her to sign over the Walking L. Now they've gone to town to get their gang of toughs. They aim to clean out the whole valley, including the Broken Wheel, using Linda as a hostage to demand surrender."

Morton twisted in the saddle. "There's the Walking L crew now. Wes Surge and Kelly are with them. They're heading for the hills to rescue Linda."

"They'd better hole up at the ranch. Make Milly and Lardey come to them."

Morton nodded. "Good idea. Let's meet them there."

The four riders got to the Walking L ranch yard ahead of the men coming up the valley. They pulled up and dismounted. In a couple of minutes the riders thundered in, the squat, heavy-set foreman of the Walking L, Sid Bodey, in the lead.

They reined up and Bodey leaned over the saddle. "What happened up there, Hudson?"

"Lardey and Milly Hayes have Linda as a prisoner," Clark said. "They're aiming to use her to make you boys surrender. Then they'll take charge of the whole valley."

Bodey's face darkened and he swore softly. "Just what did you go up there for?"

"Just for the ride," Clark snapped. "They'll be coming here with their gunslingers looking for you. You'd better get ready."

Bodey didn't move but sat stiffly in his saddle, staring at Hudson. "Maybe this is a trick to get your hands on the Walking L."

"You blithering idiot!" Nixon exploded. "You'd sit there like a fat goose in a fox den and wait till it's too late even to squawk. Clark blamed near got himself blown to bits trying to get Linda free. You're killing time that you may need."

One of the men behind Bodey spoke up. Clark recognized him as the one who had come to the Broken Wheel this morning. "He's right, Sid. We'd better get set for a fight. You know McCabe and Knox didn't pull that deal alone."

Bodey turned to look at the man, then stopped, his eyes squinting as he pointed down the valley. Clark followed his finger. A group of horsemen, too far away to number, was coming out of Antelope and heading up the valley.

"There they come," Bodey yelled, all doubt gone from his voice. "Come on. Put your horses in the corral. Let's barricade the house."

The yard suddenly erupted into a beehive of activity. Horses vanished from the front of the house. Men ran in every direction, cursing and jostling. But out of the confusion came order and a determined army of men lining the windows and doors of the house.

Clark, stationing himself close to one of the front windows, watched the oncoming riders.

CHAPTER XVII

Bodey went to the door, opened it and stood there. "What do you want?"

"Just wanted to tell you how things stand," the man said. "We've got your boss out here. If anything happens to any of us, she gets it. Understand?"

"Who said anything was going to happen to you?" Bodey countered.

"We're taking over the ranch," the man said. "It belongs to Milly Hayes and Cole Lardey."

"Since when?" Bodey bellowed, and charged out to the edge of the porch.

"Since this afternoon," the man said easily. "Linda Porter signed it over to them. Now are you going to get out?"

Bodey wheeled to the door and stuck his head inside. "Is there anything to that?" he demanded.

"He's telling the truth," Clark said. "Milly started whittling up Sam and Johnny, and she gave in and signed. Then they took her as a hostage to make you back out of a scrap."

Bodey wheeled back to the man in the yard. "Why don't you come in and take it?" he demanded belligerently.

The man laughed. "We don't have to. You'll turn it over to us without a fight if you want to see your boss alive again."

Bodey considered this a minute. "I dare you to come down off that horse and act so cocky."

The man laughed again. "I could come down. You

wouldn't lay a finger on me. 'Cause if you did, Linda gets a knife in her back. That's what Milly said when I left."

"If anybody hurts Linda, I'll boil every one of you in oil," Bodey threatened.

"You know how to keep Linda from getting hurt," the man said. "Just come out without your guns. Nobody will be hurt."

Bodey swallowed hard. "We'll think it over," he said thickly.

"Don't think any longer than fifteen minutes. That's how long Milly is giving you."

The man turned and loped his horse back to the waiting group. Bodey swore loudly as he stamped back into the house.

"He's got us where the hair's short," Bodey growled. "Looks like we'll have to give in. But once we get Linda safe, we'll tear them limb from limb."

"They'll figure that's what you've got in mind," Clark said. "Do you think you'll ever get Linda back safe? As long as they hold her, you won't dare do a thing."

Bodey stamped across the floor. "They can't hold her for ever."

"They can hold her until you and every man in your crew has left this valley. And they'll do it."

"After that they'll probably kill her," Nixon put in. "She could cause them a lot of trouble if she stayed alive."

"Then what are we going to do?" Bodey exploded.

"Hold out the fifteen minutes before you make a decision," Clark said. "I'm going to slip out through the back and get down in the barn. I just might get a chance to do something, especially if they think they've got a fight coming up. They'll try to use the barn and corrals for protection. We can't do much till we get Linda free."

"I'll take that job," Bodey said.

"You stay here," Clark said quickly. "If they want to

talk some more, it will be your job to parley with them. Stall them all you can."

Checking his gun, Clark crossed the room and slipped out the back door.

In the barn, he peered out through a crack. Fred Hayes, clinging desperately to the saddle horn, was coming slowly down the slope. Clark watched in amazement. He had been sure Hayes couldn't stay in the saddle this long.

The riders from town hadn't seen Hayes yet; they were concentrating on the man moving into the ranch yard. Then one of them looked up and shouted in astonishment.

Clark moved over where he had a wider range of vision. Milly straightened in her saddle, and Lardey cursed loudly.

"I thought you killed him," Lardey roared.

"I did," Milly said, her nerves plainly shaken.

"Well, he ain't no ghost."

Both Lardey and Milly swung up their guns as Hayes moved relentlessly forward. It was then that Linda, sitting the horse that was tied to Lardey's saddle, kicked her mount. The horse, between Lardey and Milly, lunged. The guns in Lardey's and Milly's hands roared, but the bullets went screaming into space as the riders fought to regain their balance.

Clark thrilled to Linda's spunk. But she was still a prisoner. The lead rope tying her horse to Lardey's was strong and tied securely. She had only delayed, not changed, the inevitable outcome.

By the time the riders had quieted their horses, Fred Hayes was almost upon them. He had managed to get his gun in his hand, but he was too unsteady to hold it on his target. His voice, though thick and clogged, was loud.

"I'm going to get you, Milly," he said, and aimed his horse straight at her.

Milly fired, but Hayes' shot, coming a split second

before, ruined her aim. Neither bullet scored. Then Milly's
nerve broke, and she wheeled her horse and jabbed him
with her spurs. Hayes pulled up, not trying to pursue. With
both hands he held his gun and squeezed the trigger.

Clark saw Milly's horse stumble and go down, evidently struck by the bullet. Milly, leaning far over the
saddle, had no chance to kick free. The horse hit the
ground, rolled over his rider, tried to get up and couldn't.
A close look told Clark that neither the horse nor Milly
would get up again.

He whirled his attention back to Hayes and Lardey.
Hayes, after getting off his shot at Milly, dropped his gun
and reeled in the saddle, trying desperately to hang on to
the horn with both hands. Lardey had lost his .45 when
Linda's horse had jostled his. Now he was clawing a rifle
out of his saddle boot. Levelling, it, he fired at Fred Hayes.
But he didn't hit him, for Hayes had slumped forward
and slid out of the saddle an instant before Lardey shot.
The strain of the hard ride from Abbott's old place,
climaxed by the excitement of the last few moments, had
finished the job Milly had started back in the hills.

But the booming of Lardey's big rifle had set off the
fuse. For Hayes had been between Lardey and the Walking L house, and the bullet intended for Hayes smashed
into the side of the house.

Rifles barked from the house and the riders, caught out
in the open, broke for cover. The messenger, almost to
the house, never got out of the yard. Lardey, forgetting
the threat to make Linda suffer if any shot was fired at
them, broke with his men.

Clark flattened himself against the wall of the barn as
the riders poured up the slope to the protection of the
building. The men dismounted outside, running to the
corners of the barn and corral to answer the fire from the
house.

Lardey charged past the other horses, reining up close to the door in the centre of the barn. Cursing, he dismounted.

Holding his rifle in one hand, Lardey reached up and flipped loose the knot that was holding Linda to her saddle.

"Get down," he commanded. "You're going to order your men to stop shooting."

Linda dismounted. "Now what?" she demanded.

Lardey motioned with the rifle. "Go through the barn. There must be a door on the other side where you can attract their attention and give them their orders."

Reeling forward from a shove by Lardey, Linda came into the barn. Looking neither to right nor left, she started across the barn. Lardey holding one arm. But Lardey was more cautious. His eyes shot over the gloomy interior of the structure and found Clark along the wall, waiting impatiently for a chance to move in on Lardey.

With a growling curse, Lardey circled an arm around Linda and pulled her back against him, trying to swing up the heavy rifle in his other arm.

Clark left the wall in a dive, yelling at Linda as he did so. She threw herself back against Lardey, and whatever aim he had been able to get with the heavy weapon was spoiled.

The rifle discharged, the bullet slamming into the wall ten feet from Clark. But Linda couldn't break free from Lardey's grip. He pinned her tighter, but her struggles made it almost impossible for him to do anything with the big rifle.

Clark's gun was useless, for Lardey was using the girl as a shield. Tossing the gun away, he charged forward.

Lardey had swung the gun around in front of Linda but couldn't use his other hand to get another shell into the barrel. Then, seeing that Clark had tossed away his gun, he suddenly flung Linda aside and snapped another shell into his rifle barrel. The rifle came up and roared, the bullet burning the air past Clark's ear as he came in low to grab the barrel of the rifle.

One powerful twist wrenched the gun from Lardey's hands, and Clark threw it behind him. Lardey shot one glance toward the door through which he had come, but Clark gave him no chance to run for it. Now that Milly was gone, the key to the trouble rested solely in Lardey. And Clark intended to settle the issue now.

Lardey, seeing no escape, suddenly lunged forward, fists driving into Clark. Clark retreated before the fury of the assault until he landed a counter punch on Lardey's nose that halted the storekeeper's drive. For a minute Lardey held his ground, trading punches with Clark. But he had neither the physical stamina nor the courage to stand up to Clark for long.

When he began to retreat, his eyes took on the wild desperate look of a hunted animal driven into a corner.

Lardey rocked backward, and Clark funnelled him into the entryway between the stalls. At the end of the entryway was a little side door that opened out into the front yard.

Suddenly the door latch broke and the door swung open, throwing Lardey into the yard almost in line with the fire between the corner of the barn and the house.

Clark didn't follow Lardey. He waited for the storekeeper to plunge back into the barn. But a yell went up from the house as they recognized Lardey, and a dozen rifles spoke with one voice. It seemed that an invisible hand lifted Lardey off the ground and slammed him against the door, which swung farther back, letting him slide to the ground.

Clark wheeled back to Linda, who was standing close to the back door of the barn. "Linda!"

She came running across the barn to him, and he opened his arms. She buried her head in his shirt, the tension of the last hours draining out of her in racking sobs.

"It was awful," she said.

He ran a hand soothingly over her soft hair, emotion crowding up in him. "It's over now, Linda. Were you hurt?"

She lifted her head and dabbed the tears from her eyes. "No. But Milly threatened to kill me if she didn't get her way. And she would have."

Suddenly Clark was aware that the shooting from the barn had ceased. It still continued from the house, but it was dwindling to spasmodic bursts. Then horses broke into a gallop from the barn and a volley of shots roared after them.

"They're gone," Clark said.

"What will they do now?" Linda asked, stepping back from Clark.

"Scatter. Milly and Lardey were holding them together."

Morton and Wes Surge charged into the side door. "Clark, are you all in one chunk?" Surge yelled.

"Never felt better," Clark said, moving toward the door.

The Walking L riders were swarming over the yard now, checking the results of the fight.

"Only one man nicked in the house," Morton said. "Looks like I chose the right man for the job of running the Broken Wheel."

Clark shook his head. "I don't know. I didn't prevent a fight."

Morton grinned. "Nobody could have. I was sure of that all the time. But I got the right man to handle it. I was told the day I bought the Broken Wheel there would be blood on the grass here in Porter Valley before things straightened out."

Clark thought of Milly. "She was right," he said. "But it didn't go just the way she planned."

They went into the yard where the men were milling about, excitement still in their voices.

"What about you, Miss Porter?" Morton asked, smiling wisely. "Think you'll need any help with the Walking L now?"

Linda nodded. "I could use a manager."

"You've got your foreman, Bodey," Clark suggested.

"He's just a foreman," Linda said, suddenly shy. "I need a manager, too."

Morton cleared his throat. "I think Wes will make a good foreman on the Broken Wheel."

"Hey," Clark said suddenly. "How about me?"

"You're fired," Morton said briskly. "You've done a year's work in a month. So you've earned a year's pay. Which means we're square. And, Miss Porter, that offer of a lane to the creek for your cattle still stands."

"We'll take it," Linda said quickly.

"Excuse me," Clark interrupted. "Since I'm unemployed, I've got to be looking for a job."

Taking Linda by the arm, he led her away from the bustling yard to the quiet of the prairie beyond the house.

"Now about that job of manager?" Clark began. "Do you have anybody in mind for it?"

She nodded, refusing to look at him.

"Am I too late in applying?"

"Not if you move fast."

He reached an arm around her. "Is this fast enough?"

She smiled, yielding to the pressure of his arm and moving closer to him. "I think so. It looks like you've got the job."

"I've heard that some bargains should be sealed with a kiss," he said after a moment.

"I've heard that, too," she murmured. "But I don't believe everything I hear."

"How about what you see?"

"I might believe that," she invited, looking up at him.

He accepted the invitation.